Shelly

HEARTSONG BOOKS

Shelly

Leila Prince Golding

BETHANY HOUSE PUBLISHERS

MINNEAPOLIS, MINNESOTA 55438

A Division of Bethany Fellowship, Inc.

Shelly
Leila Prince Golding

Library of Congress Catalog Card Number 85–73424
ISBN 0–87123–867–5
Copyright © 1986
Leila Prince Golding
All Rights Reserved

Published by Bethany House Publishers
A Division of Bethany Fellowship, Inc.
6820 Auto Club Road, Minneapolis, Minnesota 55438

Printed in the United States of America

Dedicated to
My Grandchildren
Who I trust
will never
have to prove
under Communism,
their love for God;

But should they . . .
May their hearts
be prepared.

Springflower Books (for girls 12–15):

Erica
Jill
Laina
Lisa
Melissa
Michelle
Sara

Heartsong Books (for young adults):

Andrea
Anne
Carrie
Colleen
Jenny
Kara
Karen
Sherri

LEILA PRINCE GOLDING brings to her second novel much experience in writing for and working with young people. Her writing credits include a weekly column for youth, articles for workers, and stories for young children. She has raised three children and worked in church youth programs. She and her husband live in northern Indiana.

Chapter One

Shelly Lee was both excited and puzzled as she left the attorney's office. Why was it so imperative for her to make the trip to Indiana as soon as possible?

She already knew that Gram had left the grandfather clock to her. Why the rush to check it?

Her large brown eyes sparkled with anticipation of the possible answer.

Mr. Baker, the attorney, had been very insistent, peering at her over his desk through the thick lenses of his spectacles.

"She left explicit instructions that you check the underside of the Schzelba drawer in the clock. Your grandmother said you would understand. Do you?"

"Oh, yes," Shelly had answered. "I understand exactly."

"Well, it certainly didn't make much sense to me," Mr. Baker had blustered, "but we meet all kinds. No offense, please, Miss Lee. Will you sign these papers, please?"

"No offense taken," Shelly said as she signed where he indicated.

"It will be best if you can go over today," Mr. Baker added, rising and moving toward the door, letting her know she was being dismissed.

"As I've told you, except for the clock, all her property and other possessions are to be sold tomorrow, with the proceeds going to her church."

"I understand," Shelly said, giving him a smile. "Thank you, Mr. Baker."

"If there's any further assistance I can offer, Miss Lee, please contact me," he said, holding the door open as he handed her a key to her grandmother's front door.

As Shelly half skipped down the steps of the old brick building housing the attorney's office, the late afternoon sun brought bright glints into her hair's long, brown loveliness.

Mr. Baker's letter setting up the appointment had arrived at her little apartment in Chicago, and she had taken time off from her job at the Center for Disabled Learners to make the short trip to his office.

I wish he hadn't given me such short notice so my substitute at the school could have taken my class an extra day. I would have enjoyed spending the night at Gram's one last time.

The drive across the border into Indiana had not taken long. As she turned her car into the street where Gram's house had stood for many decades, Shelly thought, *That house was always different; different from ours, anyway. Yet the differences were pleasant, comfortable. I always felt at home.*

As far back as she could remember, Gram had lived with Gramps in that old house in this tiny Indiana town. The small, boxy rooms and the windows that reached to the high ceilings brought back pleasant memories of fun times with Gram and Gramps.

And now she was going back, but the house would be empty. Quick tears stung her eyes as the knowledge rushed through her heart that this time Gram wouldn't be there.

But she thought of me even during her last days. Her gift of the clock proves that.

The thought warmed Shelly and her steps quickened as she brushed the tears away, remembering her joyous arrivals to this house when she was very young.

She smiled at the thought of her brother running ahead of her for Gramp's lap, scrambling for first place, squealing, "What have you got for us?" as he dug for the little toys or candy hidden for them in his pockets.

Her look softened as she recalled how they'd then turn to Gram and ask, "What have *you* got for us?"

Smiling with the joy of seeing them, she'd hold out her arms and laugh, "A big hug because I love you."

"And we would run to her," Shelly said half aloud. "Her gift, too, was satisfying to us; it was always enough."

The late sun filtered through the branches of the ancient oak, and a squirrel running up the trunk chattered crossly at her as she arrived at Gram's and walked up the short sidewalk to the wide front porch.

The inside of the house, too, was just as she remembered; except that it felt different. Shelly knew it was because of the absence of the one who had made it a home.

She found that the clock had already been crated by the movers who were to come in the morning. Its six-foot height was stretched out on its back, blanketed in plastic bubble-wrap and pads of rigid Styrofoam, the pendulum wrapped separately in bubble-wrap.

"How that bonging and that musical chiming used to startle me during the night," she remembered, recalling the beds on the couches for her brother and her during overnight visits, with her parents sleeping nearby in the guest room.

Shelly stooped down beside the crate and grasped the round, white pull on the lower left drawer of the four in the old clock.

Lifting the short, square drawer all the way out, she turned it over.

"Good, a letter," she said aloud, recalling from her childhood the notes left in that drawer.

She removed the double strip of heavy tape that secured a thick, tan envelope.

After replacing the drawer and checking the mailing tag on the crate for correctness, she ran her hand over the clock's smooth length.

"Thank you, Gram, for the memories . . . for your love."

Glancing at her watch, Shelly put the envelope deep in her shoulder bag and left the house, the door lock clicking behind her with finality.

The next morning, Shelly awoke in her apartment with a feeling of something urgent and important she had to do.

As she hurried into her little kitchen to start the coffee, she remembered.

"I was so excited and tired when I got in last night, I didn't take time to prepare the bank deposit," she scolded herself. "And I wanted to reread Gram's letter, too."

She poured herself a glass of orange juice and, before showering, got the envelope from her purse and curled up on her unmade bed.

My dear Shelly:

For many years, I have dreamed of taking a trip back to my homeland, Russia, but always there was not enough money, not enough time. Then I was too old, and too difficult the travel would have been.

But you, my dear, will you do this for me while you are still young?

Because you and I seem to believe and think much alike, I am asking you to learn about my mother country. Know some of its people. Most important of all, find out the truth about conditions under which my loved ones there live.

If true, what I hear and suspect, assist them in whatever way is possible.

I've spoken only a little about my early childhood there: of my sister, Natalia; of our grandmother Baba who cared for us after our parents' deaths.

It was Baba who started the pretending about Schzelba, that wee elf who lived who-knew-where and left small surprises for two lonely little girls.

It was her way, I think, of comforting us after our parents were gone, letting us know we had been especially good little girls and would not be forgotten by Grandfather Frost either.

Shelly smiled. "I never did decide whether I liked the name Grandfather Frost or Santa Claus best for that gentleman who visited us with such nice surprises," she reminisced.

She dropped her gaze again to the letter.

I speak of Schzelba now, not because he is important, but because the drawer he used with you is, as it has loving memories for me.

"For me, too, Gram," Shelly whispered, recalling her own experiences with Schzelba.

Then noticing the time, she realized she'd better hurry. Quickly she scanned the rest of the page.

I've sold something special I had put away for many years, in order to have this money for your trip to Russia and some extra for you to do with as you feel would be best. I wasn't feeling well enough to get this into check form. Be careful.

Quickly inserting the thick stack of hundred dollar bills into a bank deposit envelope, Shelly rushed to start her workday.

It was almost December when Shelly was finally able to arrange for a leave of absence. During the period of waiting and preparing, she busied herself with passport and visa applications. She also spent time in the library reading about the country she was to visit, corresponding with the relatives there whom she'd never met, and rereading Gram's letter.

But amidst the excitement of her preparations, Shelly recalled the frightening allusions that Gram said had been in some of her Cousin Tanya's letters, and the occasional black-outs made by censors. Shelly wondered what those words may have said.

Aunt Tanya's recent letter to her expressed delight that she was to visit them.

But even that was overshadowed with a message between the lines. In contradiction to the delight expressed was a suggestion that she might prefer, for her own sake, to delay her trip.

Shelly puzzled over that; it seemed very strange.

Chapter Two

Shelly settled herself in the comfortable seat of the train bound for Leningrad, relieved that her plane had landed in Helsinki on time for good connections.

Although excited about the trip, there was still an uneasiness concerning the unknown country ahead of her, and questions still nagging her mind.

She sighed softly, closing her eyes a moment.

"Help me, God, to discover just what Gram wanted me to accomplish."

With her dark lashes soft against her cheeks and her thick brown hair spread against the blue upholstery, she was not aware of the lovely picture she made for the young man who had sat down beside her.

She was unaware, too, that he had noticed the silent moving of her lips and the tear that slipped down the smooth roundness of her cheek.

Quickly he looked away, opening a small leather briefcase. Removing a sheaf of papers, he began jotting notes.

Half-dozing beside him, Shelly's thoughts were lost in her childhood.

"Schzelba and the clock," she said half aloud.

"Pardon?" The low, resonant voice of the man beside her broke into her reverie, startling her. Shelly jumped slightly.

She looked up to see gentle brown eyes in a strong, pleasant face gazing questioningly at her.

"I'm sorry," she smiled, embarrassed. "What did you say?"

"Well, nothing really. I thought perhaps you were speaking to me." His easy smile was questioning. "Something about the clock, I believe. Were you wanting the time?" He glanced at his watch. "It's almost . . ."

Shelly's voice trilled with soft laughter. "I didn't realize I was thinking aloud. I was recalling a clock my grandmother had and reminiscing about my childhood."

"Ah," he nodded. "And what is Schzelba?"

"Not what; who," Shelly playfully corrected him.

"Who?" the young man asked.

Then Shelly told him of the legend of the mischievous tiny elf and his escapades; the treats he'd left, and the childish notes she had left in return. The young man laughed with her at the memory of the tiny leather boot with the turned-up toe she had found early one morning near the stairs and how she had worried for weeks, fearing Schzelba had one cold foot.

"That was charming," he said.

"By the way, I'm Shelly Lee," she smiled, holding out her hand.

Laying aside the pen he was holding, he enfolded her hand in a firm, quick grasp.

"My name is Demetri Barinov. My home is in Orensk."

"Orensk!" Shelly said with delight. "That's where my relatives live. Do you possibly know a family by the name of Rozkalne on Molobka Street? Mr. Rozkalne is a welder, and his wife's name is Tanya."

A slow grin spread over Demetri's face and his eyes seemed to shine.

"I do. My mother is friends with Tanya Rozkalne. She is your aunt, perhaps?"

"My mother's cousin, but I call her aunt," Shelly answered. "How did it ever happen, do you suppose, that out of a country as vast as Russia, I should find myself seated next to someone with the same destination as mine?"

"Shelly," Demetri said softly, firmly, "God sometimes works in ways beyond our understanding. I've learned to be surprised at nothing He arranges."

He started to turn his attention back to the papers on which he had been working, but then raised his head to look again into her lovely brown eyes. "What seems a great coincidence to us may just be a part of His perfect planning."

After he had turned again to his work, Shelly pulled a small book of poetry from her purse and settled down to read.

But her thoughts kept pulling away from the music of the pages to the comments Gram had made in her letter concerning restrictions in the country that was now Shelly's destination.

The lilt and flow of the words on the pages became tangled with the questions that nagged at her.

Finally, closing the little suede-bound book, she slipped it back into the pocket in the bottom of her purse where it fit snugly against her New Testament.

Shelly ran her finger thoughtfully over the binding of the Scriptures. *I wonder,* she thought, *if it is true, as I've heard, that Bibles are in short supply, and even sometimes confiscated, in Demetri's country.*

She looked up, intending to ask him if this rumor were true, but seeing he was engrossed in what he was doing, she leaned back and turned her gaze out the window.

A lone gray-uniformed guard watched them disinterestedly as the train crossed the Finnish border and rolled through a forest of birch trees and pines.

Just ahead was a maze of barbed wire.

Shelly sat quickly upright, pressing her face close to the window as the train moved slowly into a slash of open ground reaching away in either direction as far as she could see.

"What is this place?" she asked Demetri, turning to him.

"The border of my country, the Soviet Union," he answered quietly.

Over the top of a hill ahead, Shelly saw a watchtower on stilts come into view.

Seeing that Demetri had put his work away, she voiced the concern that had been in her thoughts about the scarcity of Bibles here.

But his answer was a question.

"You are a Christian, then?" he asked very softly.

And when she nodded, her eyes looking sincerely into his, he said quietly, "Yes, it is true, Shelly."

He hesitated as though uncertain about continuing, then went on.

"My brother was arrested for printing Christian literature in his little shop. I understand the police came also to his home and ransacked it, looking for Bibles and such."

"In your own town? Why would they do that? I read just recently that your country guarantees freedom of religion for all its citizens."

"Yes, so it is written," Demetri answered, his jaw tightening, a flash of anger in his eyes, "so it is written. But life is not always what the words say it should be." Demetri shook his head abruptly. "But let us not think of that right now. Later perhaps."

The train was moving even more slowly now as it reentered woods on the other side of the barren area.

It halted and border guards in light green uniforms and high boots suddenly appeared around the train.

"They look like teenagers," Shelly said to herself, shuddering at the hip-pistols some wore and the submachine guns carried by the others.

She watched as one of them stationed himself beside the engine, while another went to stand by the rear car.

Two of the young men strode along, one on each side of the train. Shelly pressed against the window again as the guard on her side bent down to examine the undercarriages.

Heavy-booted footsteps overhead on the train's roof told her why the other two had disappeared.

Suddenly, other guards appeared in the train, going through in pairs, thoroughly searching luggage racks, the washrooms, and under the seats, while one of them checked passports.

Then almost as quickly as they had appeared, the guards were gone and the train was moving very slowly ahead.

About a mile after they had left the border, the train slowed to a crawl.

"What's the matter?" Shelly asked Demetri.

"Nothing; there's a sharp jog in the track here."

"Isn't that dangerous? Why don't they straighten it?"

Demetri laughed dryly. "It was put there purposely, so a train leaving here can't rush across the border without stopping for the mandatory inspection. The engineers going that direction know they must slow to a virtual crawl or else."

"Or else?"

"They would never make it around the jog."

As the train picked up speed again, Demetri said, "And *your* family, Shelly; what about them?"

"Well, I don't have much family anymore, Demetri," she began slowly.

"I have a brother, but he's been living in California for a while. I sometimes see him and his family during the Christmas holidays. They used to come every year, but since our folks died . . . well, they've had other plans the past few years."

"I see. And sisters, any sisters?" Demetri asked.

"No, no one else in the States except a few cousins, an aunt and uncle."

"And the relatives in Orensk, you'll enjoy being with them, yes?"

"Oh, I'm sure I will," Shelly answered, her eyes beginning to sparkle. "I've never met any of them, but my grandmother left photos and I've had a letter the past few months while I've been hoping to get away for this trip."

Demetri grinned at her. "And I'm sure they've wished for it, also. They'll not be disappointed."

Shelly smiled back, silently accepting the compliment, surprised at how at ease she felt with this man, even though they'd met only hours before. He didn't make her uncomfortable with his glances as many men did, and she liked him for that.

Later, with gorgeous colors of the sunset glowing among the scattered clouds, Shelly began questioning him tentatively about his family.

"As you know," he said, "my mother lives in Orensk. Also my sister, Galina, and her husband, Pytor Shepel. They have no children."

"Is your sister younger or older than you?" Shelly asked.

"She's older, about six years. I have an elder brother, also, Galina's twin. I mentioned him before."

Abruptly, Demetri stopped talking, his gaze turning from Shelly to the snowy distance through the window next to her.

"And where does he live?" Shelly interjected into the silence.

"I don't know . . . or even if he does."

"You don't know if he's alive? I don't understand."

"No, of course, you couldn't," Demetri said slowly. Then, "Pavel was arrested about five years ago. The authorities accused him of working against the government, I was told. They said he was printing subversive material, that sort of thing, but it was just Christian literature."

"For printing literature? But how could they do that?"

"Easily. Often they do it. There are ways. And reasons. They seem to think they're logical."

"And you have no idea where Pavel is?" Shelly asked wide-eyed.

"I've been trying to find out; soon perhaps."

Demetri's eyes held great sadness but his jaw was stern. He

shifted in his seat, clenching his hands into fists on the seat arms.

"They finally admitted that he'd been sent to a labor camp, but they would not say where. That was two years ago. Since then the family has heard nothing, except that if he is alive, we know his sentence should soon be up if they don't resentence him for some reason."

Shelly laid her hand gently on Demetri's clenched fist.

"Your family must be very concerned about him."

"Yes. Yes, we are, Shelly." His hand unclenched and turned, holding hers in a soft clasp.

"The not knowing is very difficult. We hear so many things, things that have happened to others."

"You know of others, also in prison because of Christian activities?" Shelly asked, startled.

"Yes, several personally. And there are many others. The stories come; friends from other areas occasionally get messages through. It seems many are suffering, separated from families, even tortured." Demetri kept his voice very low as he talked.

Concern evident on her face, Shelly asked, "Isn't there some way to help people who've been arrested unjustly?"

Demetri leaned back with a sigh, "There *is* no way, and most of the world evidently seems unaware. They don't seem to know, or at least don't believe, what is going on in my country. I did not myself for a long time."

"But I'm sure God knows, Demetri," Shelly said softly.

"Yes, Shelly, God knows. If that constant assurance wasn't available, there would be no hope. They would give up, having nothing to cling to."

During the rest of the ride, the things Demetri had recounted of his loved ones and friends tumbled over and over in Shelly's mind.

She wondered how she would feel if those prisoners were her friends, her family.

And she questioned whether perhaps she should not have come here.

Because she hadn't been able to sleep on the plane, she decided to try to nap when Demetri excused himself to finish his work, but her mind churned restlessly, although her body relaxed.

Demetri's hand on her arm, shaking her gently, wakened her.

"We're getting near Leningrad, Shelly. You've got just enough time to freshen up a bit, if you like."

"Thanks, Demetri," she said, sitting up more erectly and lifting her hand to brush her hair back.

She picked up her purse, and he pulled back his long legs to let her pass.

She wondered again during the time before she returned to her seat if she had been wise to take this trip. She knew Gram wouldn't have wanted her to if there actually was danger. Her uncertainty grew, but it was too late now.

Then, seated again beside Demetri, the excitement of meeting with Gram's family started mounting and she pushed the disquieting thoughts aside.

Looking out the window she watched the approaching lights across vast expanses of snow, and then suddenly the train entered a large city. Her eyes began to sparkle in anticipation.

Demetri's mirrored hers and he grinned warmly as he gave her hand a quick, gentle squeeze.

But again, as the train pulled into the station, an unexpected sense of overwhelming dread and forboding settled on Shelly.

She shivered slightly, realizing that she really was behind the Iron Curtain—an invisible curtain, yet strong and harsh as steel, about which she'd read and heard many things . . . perhaps things she'd have to reckon with.

Chapter Three

As they left the train together, Demetri said, "I'll stay with you until your family arrives to meet you."

"That's very nice of you, Demetri. Perhaps they will be waiting since we seem to be on schedule. I don't want to detain you, but I would feel better not waiting alone in a strange place."

"Then wait together it is," Demetri answered with a grin. "I have an appointment here in Leningrad before I go home, but there's plenty of time."

As they neared the customs area, he said, "Don't be tense going through. Just declare any valuables and money you have with you. Often they make a very thorough search of one's personal effects and baggage, but sometimes not."

What she had expected to be an ordeal, turned out to be a fairly routine process, and soon they stood looking around with their bags at their feet.

"You stay here a moment and I'll see if I can't find a comfortable spot in which to wait."

Demetri had scarcely spoken the words before Shelly exclaimed excitedly, "There he is; oh, I'm sure that's him!"

Demetri turned, following her gaze to where a stockily built man of medium height came bustling through the milling crowd.

Energy seemed to eminate from him, as with legs moving quickly and open topcoat flapping behind him, he rushed forward, arms outstretched.

"Shelly, our little Shelly!"

Almost before she realized what had happened, she was engulfed in powerful arms, and the smiling lips beneath a heavy black mustache had planted hearty kisses on both her cheeks.

"Uncle Vladimer! Oh, I'm so glad to see you," she said returning his hug. "Is Aunt Tanya here, too?"

"Nyet, at home she is waiting. And so excited. Never a woman so excited have you seen." He chuckled heartily.

"Well, I'm excited, too," Shelly laughed. "Uncle Vladimer, this is my friend, Demetri Barinov."

"Friend, is it?" His bushy eyebrows raised a bit as he loosened his arms from her and turned to the blonde young man who stood nearby with a smile on his face, extending his hand for a ready clasp. "From America also?"

"No, Uncle Vladimer, from Orensk. Isn't that a nice surprise?"

"Ah, yes, Barinov. Are you brother of Pavel, the imprisoned one?"

"Yes, I am."

"Yes, yes," Uncle Vladimer said a bit hurriedly. "Well, come now, little one, we must be going home."

Bending his heavy frame, he picked up her suitcases.

"These are yours, yes?"

"Yes, just those two." She turned back to Demetri, "I'll be remembering all the things you told me, about your brother especially."

"Thank you, Shelly," he said, taking her hand in both of his. "May I come by and visit you someday soon?"

"Oh, yes, Demetri, please do," she answered as she turned to follow Uncle Vladimer as he was beckoning her to leave.

The wind was brisk and cold, and Shelly was glad when Uncle Vladimer suggested they stop in a little shop where they were served glasses of hot sweet tea before going to the station.

Several hours later, their commuter train pulled into Orensk.

Shelly adjusted her scarf higher around her neck and pulled the hood of her coat snugly over her head. It had been a good decision to bring her warmest one.

The cold wind was strong against them as, leaving the station, they walked down tree-lined streets.

A couple of blocks beyond a little park, Uncle Vladimer paused before a house. "This is home, little Shelly. I welcome you."

Then, striding up to the door, he shouted, "Tanya, we are here!"

Putting down one of the suitcases, he gave several quick, powerful knocks and stepped aside for Shelly to enter.

As the door was flung open, and as Shelly stepped inside, she was engulfed with sensations.

There was the warmth of the room against her chilled face, and the aroma of something spicy baking, then the warm, caring hug of a woman in her mid-forties.

"Aunt Tanya?" Shelly asked, as the other woman stepped back, removing the apron from her ample girth and pushing a wisp of dark hair into the coil at the back of her head.

"Da, I am your dear mother's cousin. How glad we are to have you here," she said, giving Shelly another warm hug.

"Here, Vladimer," Tanya continued, "her coat. You take her coat and boots, and show her where to freshen up. Some tea, I will make."

A bit later, sipping the fragrant beverage, Shelly answered Aunt Tanya's questions.

"When my parents died a few years ago in the auto accident, I felt my plans for college were gone, and knew I would never be able to save enough for the trip here I had often thought about.

"But later," she added with a smile, "when the bank gave me the contents of my parents' safety deposit box, I discovered a letter and a bankbook."

"A letter?"

"Yes, written about six months earlier. They must have had a premonition of death. The Lord must have planned it, knowing they'd soon be gone.

Both Aunt Tanya and Uncle Vladimer watched her questioningly as she finished her tea and set the small crystal glass on the tray.

"The letter explained that the bankbook covered a special account they had started years ago in case they were no longer here when I graduated from high school." Shelly stopped a moment, biting her lip to stop its trembling.

"They said they hoped I would take two years at our local Christian college, studying basic subjects and the Bible."

"Da, is good," Aunt Tanya said softly.

"They wrote that before I continued my studies, they felt I should use as much of the money as I needed and make the trip to see you. They knew it was important to Gram and to me."

Uncle Vladimer nodded his head, an encouraging smile beneath his bushy mustache.

"But tuition had increased so much that there was little left. But Gram, too, had prepared for my trip by giving me a gift of money."

Looking from one to the other, Shelly added, "Gram's sister,

Great-aunt Natalia, may I see her now? Is she here?''

"She was taking nap," Aunt Tanya said; "I go see."

"Oh, I hope we've not wakened her," Shelly said, standing.

"No worry, child," said Uncle Vladimer. "She seems better, much better today. Yesterday, too. And happy, happy waiting for you."

Aunt Tanya reentered the room, and taking Shelly's hand said, "Come, she wants see you."

A white bun of hair topped the wrinkled face against the pillow. Dark eyes watching the doorway expectantly, began to sparkle, and a sweet smile covered her pale countenance as the little old lady lifted her arms.

"Natasha's Shelly, Natasha's Shelly."

"Aunty Natalia!" Shelly exclaimed, dropping to her knees beside the narrow bed and putting her arm over the frail shape she could barely feel through the bulky quilt.

Gently kissing the thin cheek that felt soft and fragile as a baby's beneath her lips, Shelly thought how almost transient it felt.

"I'm glad you're feeling better. You remind me so much of your sister, my gram. It is your very dark eyes, I think."

Behind her, Shelly heard Aunt Tanya translating, and she remembered that Aunt Natalia would not understand otherwise.

"It's so fortunate that you and Uncle Vladimer speak English," she said, turning.

"We learn some when our Valentina in school. She taught us. Many young people now learn English as their second language."

Getting up and sitting on the edge of the bed, clasping the hand so near the color of the sheet, Shelly looked questioningly at Aunt Tanya as Great-aunt Natalia gestured and said something.

"She wants to get up," said Uncle Vladimer, coming into the room. "You get her ready, Tanya, and to her chair I will carry her. All together we can be this night."

Although Aunt Natalia seemed to be insisting that she could walk, it was fairly obvious that she couldn't.

Shelly noticed the gentle concern in Vladimer's eyes as he picked his mother-in-law up and settled her in a chair in the next room.

He had just finished tucking a coverlet over her lap and around her feet when there was a knock at the back door.

Shelly saw a young woman enter the kitchen, followed by two youngsters bundled to their eyes against the cold.

She watched as Aunt Tanya went to help the little ones out of their coats and boots.

"Is Leonila," said Uncle Vladimer quietly, "wife of the young pastor. In prison they put him last month, and today his home they took. Everything they confiscated, everything the little family had . . . nothing left, nothing."

"They?" Shelly said, hardly understanding what she was hearing.

"The authorities. Ah, what evil. How wicked can be those who are without God," said Uncle Vladimer, rubbing his mustache thoughtfully as he shook his head.

After a moment, he called, "Little Anna, Ivan; is that you out there? Come sit by Baba Natalia. And see who else is here; Shelly from America."

In an aside, he said to Shelly, "The English Leonila says she had been teaching them this year. You can help them with it while you are here, yes?"

A sturdy boy about eight years old and a rosy-cheeked girl about six peered shyly into the room.

"Come, come little ones," Uncle Vladimer said heartily, smiling with his hand outstretched toward them.

"Come, meet Shelly."

Shelly reached into her pocket and stooped down, gravely shaking their hands, and as she did, slipping a piece of plastic-wrapped candy into each.

They backed away smiling, and skipped over to Baba Natalia's side to show her what was clasped in their fists.

Aunt Tanya stepped into the room, and after introducing the young women to each other, said, "Our Valentina's room you will share with Leonila and the children. You will not mind, Shelly?"

"No, of course not, Aunt Tanya. When will Valentina be home? Is she at work?"

After a short silence, Aunt Tanya said softly, "Next week she should be here. She was teaching children about Jesus. Her they took also."

Her eyes glistened as she looked into Shelly's. "We pray much that they will let her out after this much time. They said it is the date she would be home if she cooperates. So we hope."

"You mean," Shelly hesitated, "you mean Valentina was arrested, too?" She felt suddenly chilled, horrified.

Leonila spoke up then, "Yes, when they took my Fyodor,

Valentina and another young Sunday school teacher they took also. But I am proud of them. They did not back down as some did. Our God will sustain them."

Wiping a tear from her cheek, she added, "But I fear for Fyodor, and I miss him."

As Shelly stepped over and put her arm around the dark-haired young woman, Leonila began sobbing. "I'm so afraid for them, afraid for torture."

"Torture!" Shelly gasped. "In these modern times?"

"Da," Uncle Vladimer quietly assented, putting his arms around both of them and patting Leonila's shoulder.

"We hear sometimes, the things they do. Evil they are, evil."

Then noticing the children staring wide-eyed, he said jovially, "All of us now will be happy. We miss the Daddy Fyodor, but now we will pray. We ask God to keep him safe, to enable us be happy as we help each other."

Guiding the young women toward the huddled younsters, he said with a gentle smile, "Come, children, we join hands with Baba Natalia, all of us together."

Raising his voice so it could be heard in the kitchen, he added, "Come, Tanya, we pray."

Later, after supper, Shelly helped Leonila get the youngsters tucked into bed in the little room upstairs.

Ivan and little Anna had both given Shelly shy hugs, and she felt deeply moved at the plight of these children and their mother, who seemed only a few years older than she was.

As they turned off the light and left the room, Leonila whispered, "I am concerned also about your aunt and uncle. So kind they are to open their home to me. How they express the love of our Lord Jesus."

"Why are you concerned about them?" Shelly asked.

"The police, I heard them say when they made us leave our home, me and my children. They tell the people watching." Leonila's voice caught on a sob.

"What did they say?"

"That anyone assisting the family of the imprisoned pastor could be sent away, away to a concentration camp."

A sense of horror rushed over Shelly. "Do you think they really would?"

"Yes. We heard of it happening in another area; a year ago it was. During the night they took the father of the family. Only some food he had given, only some food."

Leonila looked at Shelly with eyes dark with fearful questioning. "Your Uncle Vladimer, this morning he told me to come here. But now I wonder. Do you think I should leave?"

"Where would you go?"

"There is no place I know of, and I fear for my Ivan and Anna." Tears slipped from Leonila's eyes.

"Don't worry," Shelly said, her arm around Leonila's shoulder, "I'm sure Uncle Vladimer realized what he was doing."

A while later, alone with Uncle Vladimer for a few minutes, Shelly said, "I don't understand why they had to leave their home."

"Often that is done to a Christian's family after he is imprisoned," Uncle Vladimer said, beginning to pace about the room. "An extra way to make him suffer, to bring him perhaps to confess to their way of thinking. Is bad, very bad."

That night, Shelly did not sleep well. She spent hours awake thinking and praying about the desperate situations she'd learned of that day.

It's like being in a different world, a world of uncertainty and fear, she thought.

Finally she fell asleep with a verse from the Bible running through her mind, "Greater is he that is in you, than he that is in the world."

Several days later, Demetri arrived early in the afternoon to invite Shelly for supper and to meet his family.

"Our phone was not working," he grinned, "but I was anxious to see you anyway."

Shortly before dusk, he returned to accompany her to his home. They walked through the tree-lined streets in the crisp cold with the snow crunching beneath their boots. Both absorbed in their thoughts, he finally turned to her and said, "Is good to be with you again, Shelly. Already I was missing you."

She smiled up at him, his erect shoulders and strong face beneath the fur hat still clearly discernible in the dusk, "And I you, Demetri. It's as though we've been friends for a long time."

"Yes," he answered, taking her hand for a moment, "and it is true in a way. For before we ever met, we were joined in Christ's love by that invisible thread that joins all Christians."

Through her mitten, Shelly felt the sudden firm pressure of his fingers, a token of that closeness, that special friendship that can surpass others. Her heart felt warm and very happy.

Several hours later, after a comfortable evening of visiting in his home, they retraced their steps through darkness, now softened by a full moon. The snow glistened in the soft light, making Shelly's heart sing with its beauty and the joy she felt at the presence of the young man striding along beside her.

He left her at the Rozkalnes' front door after it had been opened at his knock. But before he turned to go, he thanked her again for coming to see his family, adding that he would see her again soon.

Uncle Vladimer was sitting close to his short-wave radio, gently turning the dial. Aunt Tanya and Leonila sat near Great-aunt Natalia mending the children's clothes.

Shelly greeted them and gave Aunt Natalia a hug. "She's up later tonight," she said, looking at Aunt Tanya.

"Yes, she insisted. Her eyesight, it is not good; but hearing she does fine. The program this night, she enjoys much. God's Word, it is. Channelled to us from stations sponsored in America. Several such we get each week. A blessing they are."

Leonila looked up after cutting a thread and turning the sock right side out. "Yes, is a blessing being together in this way, too, listening to words of—"

She stopped abruptly as Natalia, from her chair in the corner nearest the door, made a shushing sound, her finger to her lips.

Quickly, Uncle Vladimer turned the radio off. They could hear the movements outside on the walk.

The heavy footsteps stopped outside the door. There was no knock; just silence.

Swiftly Uncle Vladimer rose from his chair and walking softly across the room, peered carefully through a crack between the drapes and shutters.

Face tense, finger to his lips, he stepped to Tanya's side, "Druzhinniki," he whispered.

"Civilian deputy," Leonila whispered to Shelly.

Uncle Vladimer put a hand on Leonila's arm, "And with him a policeman."

Pulling her gently, but firmly, to her feet, he whispered urgently, "Upstairs, quickly."

He bent to pick up a fallen sock, "The little ones' clothes, take them with you."

Hurriedly gathering up the things from his wife's lap, too, he shoved them at Shelly. "Here, you take; also you go. Quickly, quickly upstairs!"

Chapter Four

Quietly, quickly, Shelly and Leonila crept up the narrow stairway to the bedside of the sleeping children.

Leonila crouched on the edge of the bed, then dropped to her knees, praying silently.

With the bundle of children's clothes still clasped against her chest, Shelly tiptoed to the small window.

Peering between the worn curtains with her forehead pressed against the frosty glass, she could see the area near the front door and the two figures just barely in her line of sight, dark against the snow.

One of them raised an arm as though to knock, then stopped in midair, dropping it to his side.

Turning, they crossed the street and walked on out of sight.

"They've left," Shelly stated, her voice trembling with relief. Calling quietly to the others downstairs, she told them the crisis was past.

"Thanks be to God," Leonila whispered, getting to her feet. She leaned over the bed, tucking the covers around Anna and Ivan.

"They may suspect I'm here," she said dejectedly. "What shall I do, Shelly; what shall I do?"

"I don't know, Leonila. I've never been in a situation like this before," Shelly admitted, putting her arm around Leonila's shoulder.

"But for now, let's go to bed, trusting Uncle Vladimer to know what he's doing, and God to watch over us, giving us safety for the night."

Leonila nodded, "I'm glad you're here, Shelly. It's nice to have a friend near my own age in addition to the others downstairs. They are so good to me and risking their own safety to express God's love."

"I guess that's what Christians are supposed to do," Shelly said, "but I never dreamed I'd have to confront a situation like this. It's hard to realize it is really happening to someone I know."

"I hope that's the closest it comes to you, Shelly," Leonila said quietly, removing her sweater.

Shelly lay awake a long time pondering the happenings of that day. She prayed for the safety of this little family, for Leonila's husband in prison, for cousin Valentina, for Demetri's brother.

Then several hours before dawn, she fell asleep thinking of Demetri's soft brown eyes and gentle manner.

The sun was shining through the flimsy curtains at the little window when Shelly woke and turned over.

Ivan, Leonila's little boy, was standing near the foot of the bed, staring solemnly at her.

"Breakfast," he said.

"Breakfast is ready?" she asked with a smile.

Ivan nodded, and having delivered his message, he ran out of the room.

Shelly hurriedly dressed and straightened her bed.

In the kitchen she found Aunt Tanya dishing up bowls of hot cereal, while the children scampered around the table giggling.

When the meal was finished and the women were lingering over their tea, Aunt Tanya asked, "Shelly, would you care to go with me shopping?"

"Yes, I'd like that," Shelly answered.

Later that morning at the market they were standing, last in a long line, waiting to purchase a bit of meat when an elderly gentleman with downcast eyes shuffled toward the back of the line.

He was moving slowly as though his feet hurt, and Shelly thought he intended to get in line behind her, but he started to pass.

As he did, the small bundle he was carrying fell to the ground.

Before she could stoop to retrieve it for him, he bent to pick it up. As he did so, she saw his gaze lock with Aunt Tanya's for a moment.

There was no sign of recognition in their eyes, but as he stood up and shuffled away, she heard him whisper, "Ten."

Shelly's curiosity was roused, but Aunt Tanya continued to chat casually about insignificant things.

It was during supper that evening that Shelly discovered the encounter had not been by chance.

The youngsters had finished eating and were permitted to leave the table. Leonila had cautioned them to play quietly, and Shelly could hear them chattering over some small toys in the living room.

"We go out tonight," Aunt Tanya said quietly.

"Ah, is good," Uncle Vladimer said. "Where?"

"Victor Belan's, ten o'clock," she answered softly.

Uncle Vladimer nodded; then leaning across the table, he said, "Shelly, our church meets in secret this night. You are welcome to join us. You will come, yes?"

"Yes, Uncle Vladimer, I'll be happy to. But why in secret? I don't understand."

"Ah, Shelly, our church building was locked by the authorities since they arrested our pastor and our Valentina. We are not allowed to use it, so they think they have defeated us."

"Why did they do that?"

"We are not a registered church. Also a Bible school for the children we had, and that was not acceptable. Many of the little churches have been closed."

Uncle Vladimer sighed, "They may open it again and install a new pastor, someone who will cooperate in enforcing the laws regarding religion, as they did in several nearby towns."

"Would it not be a Christian man?" Shelly asked.

"Ah, yes, the Lord's children they are, usually. But they are afraid; they do whatever they are told to."

He reached over and patted Shelly's hand, "But we must not feel harshly toward them. Some have been worn down by threats and feel they cannot resist anymore. Others are not fully aware of the treachery of what they are asked to do.

"Why not register? they think. What harm is there in listing our members and reporting who was saying what?"

Uncle Vladimer pushed his chair back, "They don't realize that later it may be used against them."

He stood up, "I must go now; is starting to get dark."

After slipping into his heavy coat and pulling a large fur hat down over his ears, he put his arms gently around Tanya, "One hour, you and Shelly. Go by Street Number Four to Ronski. I will go the longer way."

Turning to Leonila, he put his arm around her shoulder. "You stay, you and the little ones with Baba Natalia. Safer it is. We will share with you when we return."

Uncle Vladimer pulled on his overshoes and opened the back door. A great gust of cold wind blew across the kitchen before he could pull it closed behind him, and Shelly shivered.

"Is getting much colder," Aunt Tanya said. "You need not go if you would rather not, Shelly."

"No, I want to attend the meeting with you," Shelly said. The excitement of a secret meeting was enticing to her, though she wondered if the secrecy was really necessary.

Then she remembered why Leonila and her children were here and her heart quaked.

Before leaving, Shelly went in to Aunt Natalia's room to tell her good night.

She smiled at Shelly, saying something, and Aunt Tanya repeated, "She wants you to know again how happy she is that you're here. Also, she's pleased that you are going along to the meeting and will be praying for us."

Shelly bent to kiss Aunt Natalia's cheek and pat her hand, wishing she had gone to see Gram more.

As they left the room, she turned to Aunt Tanya. "Thank you for interpreting for me. I appreciate it, too, that you always speak English when I'm around."

"We want you to be at home here, to feel part of our family."

"I do," Shelly said earnestly. "The only difficulty I'm having is trying to understand the persecution some Christians are facing. It would make sense if they were enemies of some sort causing your country problems. I'm not meaning to offend you, but I just can't comprehend your government's attitude."

They were walking through the kitchen, fastening their coats. Leonila was putting away the dishes she had just washed, and she answered Shelly's comment.

"Do you remember the verse in the Bible, 'Father, forgive them; they don't know what they're doing'? So it is, I believe, in our country."

Turning to Tanya, she said, "I know you must be going; explain to her on your way, yes?"

"Of course," Aunt Tanya answered, giving Leonila a quick hug before she opened the door.

The wind was biting cold as they walked to a back street. Shelly noticed that the full moon of the night before had begun to wane.

"Is good we have plenty of time," Aunt Tanya whispered. "We must stay in shadows when we can and go as quietly as possible."

But Shelly feared there was no way to avoid the loud sound of crunching snow beneath her feet until she noticed Aunt Tanya's gliding stride that swept her boot across the surface of the snow and let the toe of her boot sink into the whiteness first, followed almost soundlessly by the heel.

Shelly tried it, and after a few clumsy steps found it to be not tiring as it had at first appeared.

As they turned onto another street, Aunt Tanya said softly, "What Leonila was saying is true. We live under a government that is atheistic, denying God. So the people are instilled from early youth with unbelief in Him.

"Christian activities and churches not registered with the government and controlled by them are considered anti-government and treated so."

Aunt Tanya continued, "The police and prison guards don't realize that in mistreating Christians, they are acting against Almighty God. In their eyes, I suppose, they are just upholding the law.

"But it is a law against the God who created them. Difficult as it seems to do so, we must pray for them."

"But, don't you hate them for what they've done to Valentina and the others?" Shelly asked, trying to keep her voice low.

"No, I don't hate them anymore. At first, yes; my heart was angry and very hard toward them."

Aunt Tanya took Shelly's arm, guiding her to a turn into another street.

"But Vladimer reminded me that God's Word tells us to pray for those who despitefully use us. I forced myself to at least voice the prayers; soon the hate and the anger began to melt away and I saw them as misguided, lost people."

"I suppose so," Shelly agreed grudgingly.

"The Lord loves them and doesn't want them to perish eternally, Shelly. Jesus died for them as He did for us."

As they moved quietly through the snow-covered streets, Shelly wondered whether she could be that forgiving, even though God said she should.

"Remember, too," Aunt Tanya continued, "Jesus said we should pray that the Heavenly Father would forgive us our own sins in the way we forgive the sins of others."

Shelly nodded, but said nothing, wondering if there shouldn't be exceptions to what we were expected to forgive.

They were almost at the end of this street when Aunt Tanya took Shelly's arm again, whispering, "Say nothing."

Shelly nodded and stopped with her in front of a completely darkened house.

Aunt Tanya bent as though to adjust her boot, glancing quickly in both directions before she rose.

"Try to step in the footprints already leading to the door," she whispered.

Aunt Tanya linked her arm through Shelly's to steady them both in the deep snow as they approached the door. Without knocking, Aunt Tanya opened the door and led Shelly inside.

It seemed to Shelly that it was almost as dark indoors as out.

A very small lamp in a corner of the next room was the only illumination, but a hand reached out from the shadows and they were led to a space on a couch.

"We'll keep our boots on and our coats with us," she said softly.

As Shelly's eyes became accustomed to the light level, she saw that there were about a dozen people seated around the room, some with heads close together in whispered conversation, others with heads bowed, evidently praying.

Shelly followed Aunt Tanya's lead in removing her coat, then sitting with it bundled on her lap.

Shelly's gaze followed the perimeter of the room and she saw Uncle Vladimer through the door near the lamp.

Shelly shivered when a cold blast of air struck her as the door opened to admit another couple. She saw to her delight that the taller one was Demetri. Aunt Tanya held out her hand as she and Shelly moved to make room between them for Galina.

Although none of the three women spoke, there were hugs of greeting.

Demetri gave Shelly's shoulder a gentle squeeze and smiled through the gloom before seating himself on the floor at her feet.

About ten minutes later the door opened again as someone else arrived. In this manner, the people gathered throughout the evening until the two rooms became very crowded, with people seated on every piece of furniture as well as all available space on the floor.

No one seemed to mind the press in the quiet dusk, but Shelly was glad the weather was not hot. She realized the discomfort they must feel when it was.

Someone near Uncle Vladimer began speaking. Shelly recognized him as the elderly man who had passed the meeting-signal to them earlier that day at the market.

Aunt Tanya translated quietly as he spoke in a quiet, quavering voice.

"In the name of our Lord and Savior, Jesus Christ, I welcome you into my home. May the presence of His Spirit fill our hearts as we worship Him."

The old gentleman then wended his way carefully between the people seated on the floor to the door and locked it.

A woman to Shelly's right began to hum and soon others joined in with a few singing very softly.

The tune was familiar to Shelly's ears and she joined in softly singing.

Praise Him, Praise Him,
Jesus our blessed Redeemer. . . .

The singing of several other hymns followed, hushed in volume, but filling the room with a resonance that seemed to vibrate in Shelly's heart.

She felt awed by the calmness in this group of God's children who proclaimed their praise and trust in Him in the midst of trying times.

Then as the last notes of "God, Our Help in Ages Past," melted into quietness, a hush fell over the room.

Minutes later, as though a command had been given, hands were reached out to join with those of others nearby until all were joined in a gesture of oneness.

One of Shelly's hands was held by Aunt Tanya, and she felt the firm, but gentle clasp of Demetri's strong hand on her other.

From the far side of the room, someone began to pray quietly.

Although Shelly couldn't understand the language of the phrases, she felt the deep sincerity with which they were spoken.

When the person praying stopped, another began, and Aunt Tanya put her forehead against Shelly's hair and softly translated into her ear the words the various voices were uttering.

Shelly's eyes began to sting with tears as she realized how many of the prayers consisted of praise and thanking the Lord.

The only requests were those for strength to endure the persecution they and the imprisoned ones might face; that they be able to love instead of hate; above all, that they not deny the One who had died to save them.

Shelly thought with embarrassment of her past "give-me, do-for-me" prayers and knew that after this evening, she could never again have such a casual approach in her conversations with God. She felt ashamed of her self-serving attitude when talking to her Heavenly Father.

Mrs. Barinov, Demetri's mother, had just finished praying when into a silence filled with the awareness of God's presence came heavy footsteps outside followed by a sharp knock at the door.

Around the room, clasped hands tightened and hearts raised quick petitions to the Lord.

Shelly held her breath, knowing everyone else was probably doing the same as they asked God's protection.

Chapter Five

The knocks were repeated, louder and more demanding this time, followed by the sounds of two men in angry conversation.

A fist pounded on the door again, then rattled the knob.

Then the voices came again, but calmer now, followed by the sound of footsteps retreating into the distance.

The little congregation corporately held its breath, then sighed together a rush of whispered thanks to God.

The old gentleman, Victor Belan, quietly unlocked the door, admitting rushes of icy air as he cautiously peered outside.

Closing it with a smile, he nodded toward Uncle Vladimer who was helping two women put on their coats.

They reached out, touching hands of others in the rooms as they made their way to the door and departed.

Half an hour later, someone else left. In pairs or alone, the worshipers began dispersing every ten minutes or so, until about half of them had gone.

"You go, now," Uncle Vladimer said softly, joining Shelly and Tanya.

Demetri got up from his place on the floor where he had been talking quietly to them and helped Shelly with her coat.

"Our God go with you," he whispered as she turned and followed Aunt Tanya through the semi-darkness to the door.

The wind seemed much colder than it had earlier and Shelly pulled her hood close around her face, tucking her chin into the collar as she stepped carefully into the bootprints leading from the door to the main walkway.

Leonila was still up, alone in the kitchen when they arrived. She took an already steaming kettle and quickly prepared tea.

The three were sitting at the kitchen table when Uncle Vladimer arrived much later and joined them for a cup of the hot, comforting drink.

"All went well," he said, smiling. "I was the last to leave this night. Sure I am that I saw someone standing in the shadows near the corner of Ludlow Street, but I could not make out who it was."

He took several sips of his tea, sighing with satisfaction at its warmth. "On Saturday night we gather in the old barn at the north edge of town. Victor's place not safe for a while, I think."

"I'll stay with the children, Leonila," Tanya said, "so you may have the strength of fellowship."

Shelly said, "Let me do it, Aunt Tanya."

"No, Shelly, dear. Thank you for your thoughtfulness, but I want you to know the pressures many of our people face, so you will remember when you are home in America, and will tell others."

Saturday evening arrived crisply cold and clear. The children, Anna and Ivan, had been fed and tucked in for an early bedtime.

As she and Leonila started back downstairs, Shelly noticed the thick coating of frost and ice covering the window panes.

She thought of the cold walk she would be taking later with Leonila to the gathering of believers and wondered if they would confront the possibility of danger again.

Downstairs in the kitchen, they joined the two other adults for a supper of the black-bread soup Shelly was learning to relish.

Uncle Vladimer smiled at them, "Glad I am that there has been no new snowfall or our tracks would be much more noticeable."

"I'm glad, too," Shelly thought. Although there was an undercurrent of excitement in the danger involved in the clandestine services, she hoped she would not have to face the reality of apprehension.

"I wonder what I'd do, what my reactions would be, if the meeting was actually interrupted by the police," she questioned herself.

At dusk, after they were bundled into their warmest clothes with an extra layer underneath, Uncle Vladimer said, "You two go out the front door. Turn left at the second corner and keep walking until I meet you.

"I will go another way from here."

Aunt Tanya had told them that they need not try to be unobtrusive until after they had met Uncle Vladimer, that until then it was all right to chat as they walked together.

So Leonila talked quietly to Shelly, telling her of the village church her husband had served as pastor after the disappearance of the man who had presided there for many years.

"He disappeared? Have you located him?" Shelly asked.

"No," Leonila answered. "The authorities had been pressing the church to register. They were to list the members and limit the meetings and what could be preached."

"And the church wouldn't register, from what Uncle Vladimer said."

"They all agreed not to, as did we when we arrived. We wished to worship God as He led, not as men commanded, especially men who did not know Him."

"Do you think the authorities had something to do with the man's disappearance?" Shelly asked.

"Oh, yes. They were planning to put one of their choosing in charge. But when he arrived the next Sunday, my Fyodor was in the pulpit.

"He calmly and courteously refused to let the other man take over. There was only one plain-clothes policeman with him and he was unarmed, so there was no real problem. They just sat in the service with the rest of us."

"Then why is Fyodor in prison? What happened?"

"All went well for two weeks, although we felt sure that at least one of the new people in the congregation was Secret Police or one of their spies."

"Weren't you afraid?" Shelly asked.

"Yes, I was. I knew something could happen to Fyodor. And eventually, they came and took him."

"How did it happen?"

"It was a Sunday morning. He was teaching the adult Bible class when the door opened and four armed men came in. Two of them marched down the aisle and forced him to leave with them."

Leonila stopped talking as they approached the second corner where they were to turn.

The street they entered was deserted except for several people on the other side headed in the opposite direction.

"I hurried down the aisle after them, as did several others, and asked where they were taking him. They didn't answer but forced us back with their guns.

"The other two men had burst through the door into the adjacent room where your cousin, Valentina, and another woman were teaching the children. They arrested them also."

"It's difficult to realize," Shelly said, thinking of the Sunday school classes at home that were taken so for granted.

"What were the girls charged with?" she asked.

"Involvement in activities against the State. They accused Fyodor of teaching dangerous subversive doctrines."

A figure approached in the gathering darkness from a side street, so both young women became silent as they hurried along.

The other person soon came abreast of them and Shelly recognized the stocky outline just before he spoke, "I will be about a block behind you on the other side of the street."

"Oh, Uncle Vladimer," Shelly said in a hushed voice full of relief.

"Take old Pine Road at the edge of town, Leonila," he said, as he passed them. "Enter the barn at its south end. There's a small door at the back."

Shelly felt more relaxed knowing Uncle Vladimer was so close by. She linked her arm with Leonila's as they hurried along in the dark. Their footprints mingled with those of many others made since the last snowfall.

It didn't seem to Shelly that the rest of the walk to the edge of town took very long. She found that beyond them to their left was a vast field. Near its edge, several blocks away, was a dark shape that she supposed would be their destination.

Leonila stood quietly a few moments, glancing in all directions. Shelly did also, determining that the area seemed deserted.

But she couldn't see Uncle Vladimer either, though he was supposedly not far behind them. The realization made her uncomfortable.

"Come," Leonila whispered, pressing Shelly's arm against her side.

They didn't go directly to the building that was dark against the soft glow of the snow-covered landscape. Instead, they started across the field at an angle away from it, and curved their path back toward it.

Shelly had her chin tucked in her collar, her head down against the cold wind, letting Leonila partially lead her.

She realized suddenly that the dark shape in the distance had materialized into a large building looming just before them.

They heard no sounds except their own breathing and the crunch of snow beneath their boots. Shelly supposed they must be the first ones to arrive.

They found the door on the back wall just around the corner, and Leonila pulled it open.

The grating noise of the stiff rusty hinges seemed excessively loud to Shelly, and she glanced around nervously before following Leonila inside.

Quiet coughing and the clearing of several throats was startling in the darkness. Shelly jumped, but she was glad they were not alone. Perhaps the wait wouldn't be very long tonight. The building was obviously unheated and it was very cold.

Shelly thought, as she had the other evening, of churches at home, warm and bright with carpeting and upholstered pews. She wondered how many of the people she attended church with would be willing to gather together as these folks were doing, especially in a place as unlikely as this one.

Another couple entered a few minutes later, followed by Uncle Vladimer.

Someone flicked a flashlight on for just a moment, pointing out a low pile of hay.

Shelly and Leonila seated themselves on the soft springy mass next to several other ladies, and were joined by the couple who had arrived just after they did.

She could barely make out Uncle Vladimer making his way to the middle of the room guided briefly by the flashlight held by someone at one side of the spacious room.

A sudden glow appeared in the room's center as Uncle Vladimer lit a candle, revealing an area of bare wood floor on which stood a weathered crate. It's top held a worn Bible on a square of white cloth.

In a glass was the candle stub which cast the circle of light.

Shelly could now see in the darkness of the room's perimeter a large number of people, many more than she had expected.

Uncle Vladimer lifted his hands, looking upward, and Leonila translated softly in Shelly's ear as he prayed.

"Our God, we have been meeting in homes this week to praise and worship You. We come together this night to listen to You.

"Open the ears of our hearts as we hear Your Word read. May we individually and as a group discern what You are saying to us.

"And give us, Lord, the strength and the wisdom each of us may need in the coming days. Amen."

Uncle Vladimer bent forward to open the Bible on the low crate.

Shelly watched wonderingly as with difficulty because of his size and the bulkiness of his coat, he knelt, supporting himself with his hands on the crate.

Pulling the candle closer to the book, he pulled some spectacles from an inner pocket and put them on, carefully fitting the wire temples over his ears.

Shelly sensed the attitude of expectancy in the room as the group waited for him to begin reading; she marvelled at this, never before had she experienced an atmosphere like this in a service.

It's similar to the feeling a crowd has before an important ball game, she thought, *or waiting for the opening curtain of a great play.*

As though reading Shelly's thoughts, Leonila whispered, "Except for a few Bibles members have secreted, that is the only one in our entire church."

Startled, Shelly turned to her and Leonila continued, "I will tell you more about this later."

Uncle Vladimer slowly turned some pages, then looking around with a smile said, "Hear God's Word." His voice was strong and clear as he began to read.

Shelly clasped Leonila's hand in gratefulness as she began again to translate in a soft whisper.

The Lord is my shepherd; I shall not want.
He maketh me to lie down in green pastures:
He leadeth me beside the still waters.
He restoreth my soul: He leadeth me in the paths of
    righteousness for his name's sake.
Yea, though I walk through the valley of the shadow of
    death,
I will fear no evil;
For thou art with me.

That's what these people are doing, Shelly thought, *walking through a place where death shadows them.*

She was lost in thought about her own priorities as she heard Uncle Vladimer's and Leonila's voices in the background.

Later, while Uncle Vladimer again turned pages to another passage, several elderly people moved closer to the center of the room, cupping a hand to their ears as others assisted them in re-seating themselves.

When Uncle Vladimer had finished several more passages, he said, "And from the ninety-second psalm, two verses."

It is a good thing to give thanks unto the Lord, and to sing praises unto thy name, O most High. To show forth thy loving-kindness in the morning, and thy faithfulness every night.

Someone began singing softly; others joined the gradually swelling music of voices.

Shelly recognized the melody even before Leonila began singing in English.

What a friend we have in Jesus,
All our sins and griefs to bear.
What a privilege to carry
Everything to God in prayer.

Shelly's sweet alto joined the others as they continued, singing another verse:

Oh, what peace we often forfeit,
Oh, what needless pain we bear,
All because we do not carry
Everything to God in prayer.

Following the singing of several more songs, there was a short silence broken by the voice of a man near Shelly. "I want to thank our God for the privilege of meeting here this night."

Leonila translated this and the few sentences of thanksgiving spoken by several others.

Then, as a woman spoke from the other side for the room, Leonila gasped and grabbed Shelly's arm.

"What is it, Leonila?" Shelly whispered, "What's wrong?"

"Nothing's wrong. Oh, Shelly, that is Olga. She was arrested with my Fyodor. She said she got home just today. I must speak to her after the service."

"Oh, I thank God. Fyodor and Valentina will probably be home soon, too."

"I'm so happy for you, Leonila, and for Aunt Tanya and Uncle Vladimer." Shelly gave her a hug, though sitting in the hay, wearing heavy coats, it was difficult and they both giggled, but quieted quickly.

Uncle Vladimer was slowly turning pages again in the silence. Then looking around with another smile which cast strange shadows across his face in the candlelight, he laid the book down on the crate, removed his spectacles and wiped his eyes while a murmur of voices began to flow around the room for a brief minute.

Replacing his spectacles, he resumed reading.

"The book of Mark," Leonila whispered to Shelly.

Shelly thought, *Surely, he didn't mean the entire book of Mark. There must be ten or twenty chapters in it.*

But the entire book is what Uncle Vladimer had meant. He made no comments nor tried to give his interpretation of the Scriptures he was reading. He just delivered them in a distinct, evenly paced voice.

After a while, Shelly realized her legs and feet were getting very cold, so she pulled some of the sweet-smelling straw over them, pushing her feet deep into the pile as she had noticed the lady next to her doing in the gloom.

Though it left several sprigs of straw sticking from the wool of her mittens, it warmed her like a fluffy quilt.

As Leonila shifted her position, leaning easily against her, Shelly felt sympathy for the burden Leonila carried on her heart because of her husband.

Returning her attention to Uncle Vladimer's and Leonila's voices, she recognized the chapters being read; she'd heard them in portions in church all her life and had read them herself during her daily times of prayer and Bible reading. But never before had she read or heard the entire book at one time.

Occasionally someone coughed, but mostly all was silent under the sound of Uncle Vladimer's voice, except for soft rustlings as folks shifted their positions, and the sound of Leonila's translating.

So then, after the Lord had spoken unto them, he was received up into heaven, and sat on the right hand of God.

The candle was sputtering, about to be put out by its own liquid wax.

A flashlight was turned on and the person holding it got up and went to stand by the crate in the center of the room, shining it on the book between the hands of the kneeling reader.

Uncle Vladimer quickly but gently turned the pages to the very back of the book; as he read again, Shelly recognized Leonila's words as from the book of the Revelation:

> Blessed are they that do his commandments, that they may have right to the tree of life, and may enter in through the gates into the city.

There was a pause, then:

> He which testifieth these things saith, surely I come quickly. Amen. Even so, come, Lord Jesus. The grace of our Lord Jesus Christ be with you all. Amen.

Uncle Vladimer wrapped the Bible in the white cloth, and, standing with much effort, handed it to another man who had come forward.

He opened his coat and placed the Bible inside his sweater, which was tucked into the top of his pants.

After quickly buttoning his coat, he put his arms around Vladimer, patting his back. Then going to the door, the man turned the flashlight off and peered out into the starry night. As he stepped outside, everyone was absolutely silent, listening.

He returned in a few minutes, closed the door and turned his light on.

Immediately Uncle Vladimer raised his hands in benediction and asked God's blessing upon His Word in their lives.

The light was switched off, and when Uncle Vladimer had said amen he began singing softly; Leonila's voice joined his in English.

Soon the large cold expanse of the barn was filled with a melody that always brought a tingle to Shelly's spine when she heard it:

> God be with you 'til we meet again,
> By His counsels guide uphold you,
> With His sheep securely fold you:
> God be with you 'til we meet again.

Tears stung Shelly's eyes as she realized that these people were singing with the knowledge of the possibility that they would not meet again in this way.

They are like soldiers in the middle of a big battle, she thought.

During the soft singing, the flashlight had been flicked on for a few moments, and a woman had gotten up from the straw and joined the man at the door.

The light went off, he opened the door, revealing again the

expanse of stars; they went out into the night.

Someone had lit a candle stub and placed it on the crate so the darkness inside the barn was once again turned to a dusk in which people could vaguely see one another

"Excuse me, Shelly," Leonila said, pushing herself up from the straw. "I must talk with Olga. She may know something about Fyodor and Valentina."

As Leonila crossed the room in the gloom, Shelly noticed several more people leaving.

She heard the stirring of the straw as someone approached from behind and dropped down beside her.

"Hello, Shelly."

Her heart seemed to leap with happiness, "Demetri! I'm so glad you're here. I hadn't known whether to expect you, but thought I saw you enter. When you began singing, I felt sure it was you."

Shelly smiled at him, "This was the most unusual meeting I've ever attended."

"Yes, we meet in some strange places at times, but often we feel the police are watching our usual gatherings once they find where they are located, and know they may break up the meeting.

"There seem to be some especially anti-Christian men in this area at present."

Shelly recalled the men at Uncle Vladimer's door, and Victor Belan's. She was beginning to realize more and more that there were real problems here.

"I would very much like to walk home with you, Shelly. I came here alone. Shall I ask your uncle if this is all right?"

Just as Demetri started toward the small group near Uncle Vladimer, Shelly saw Leonila coming toward her. She got up to meet her, brushing clinging straw from her clothes.

"Oh, Shelly!" Leonila exclaimed, throwing her arms around her, "In two days Valentina may be home. That gives me much hope that Fyodor will come sooner than the long months, perhaps years, that we had expected."

"I'm so glad," Shelly responded, hugging her back. "Ivan and Anna will be excited when they hear this."

"So happy I am that I came tonight. And so excited. I've heard nothing until now, and wasn't allowed to visit.

"Olga said she and Valentina were called together into an office this morning where they were told they would be released day after tomorrow.

"Then late this afternoon, a guard came for Olga, telling her to bring her things. He took her to the main gate and told her she was free to go.

"She doesn't know why this happened."

"That is strange," Shelly said. "I wonder why they didn't release Valentina at the same time?"

Leonila put her hand on Shelly's arm. "I saw Demetri leaving you, going toward Vladimer. If you would like to walk with him, I will go with Olga's family. I would like to ask more questions."

"Thanks, Leonila. See you at home."

"Remember to have him take you in the back way. He will know which streets to use."

Shelly stood alone, picking remaining pieces of straw off her coat and slacks, watching as more people left every few minutes.

A small group of people clustered around Uncle Vladimer and the young woman Shelly supposed was Olga.

Demetri stood near them, waiting to speak to Uncle Vladimer.

After Leonila left with two women, she noticed that except for the small group in the center of the barn, most of the worshipers were gone.

Shelly shifted from foot to foot, the cold beginning to penetrate her clothes now that there weren't people close by.

She pulled her hood more tightly around her face and tucked her chin under the collar, hoping Demetri would hurry.

She noticed the candle stub beginning to sputter and Demetri approaching Uncle Vladimer as another couple went out the door into the deeper darkness.

They all heard it at once. The screech of brakes . . . vehicle doors opening and shutting . . . the sound of men's voices.

Shelly saw Uncle Vladimer reach forward to snuff the candle, and Demetri sprinting toward her.

Finding her mittened hand in the darkness, he half-dragged her as he plowed through the straw to the corner of the barn.

She stumbled and fell headlong as he pushed her down.

"Hurry! Burrow under the straw. Hide yourself!" he whispered sharply.

Shelly struggled frantically to comply as he piled straw on top of her. Then she felt him burrow in beside her, and heard the swishing of the straw as he tried to conceal himself.

Chapter Six

Shelly lay against the rough wood of the barn's wall, on the side of the building facing the road.

She moved away slightly, letting a layer of straw fall between the wall and her to cut the intense cold.

"Don't move!" Demetri's whisper was somewhere near her head. "Stay completely still."

Shelly was lying on her left side, facing the wall, her head pillowed on her right hand. A cold wind blew against her cheek.

Moving so slowly that the straw made no sound, she very carefully poked her mittened fingers through the mass of straw.

Carefully, inch by inch, she made a tiny tunnel to a crack in the board through which the wind was filtering.

Straining her gaze through the narrow space, she saw approaching flashlights.

Suddenly one of them bobbed across the field. There were shouts, and the sound of running feet outside converging on the barn.

"I can see through a crack, Demetri," she whispered. "I think they're chasing someone."

"I thought so," he whispered back. "Quiet now; they will probably come in."

Proving his prediction, she saw two figures, carrying lights, pass just outside where she and Demetri lay hidden. The men rounded the corner, heading for the back of the barn.

Shelly felt the firm pressure of Demetri's hand, reassuring her.

She heard the rattle of the door latch and the sudden loud rasp of the hinges as the door was violently thrown open.

Shelly jumped as it hit the wall. Demetri gripped her shoulder as hard as he could, cautioning and steadying her.

Then came the echoing sound of heavy boots on the floor and harsh voices talking together.

Shelly heard the crate being toppled and the crash of the candle-holder as it smashed on the bare floor.

There were repeated thudding-scraping sounds. Shelly wondered if one of the men were climbing up the ladder to the loft. When she heard the thud of heavy steps overhead, she knew her guess had been right.

Soon the muted scrape of his steps returning down the ladder penetrated her straw cover.

Then through the darkness of her enveloping cocoon came a loud metallic twang and a thud of wood bouncing against wood. Shelly remembered seeing a pitchfork standing against the wall and supposed it must have been knocked over.

One of the men said something, followed by the hard laughter of both of them.

The thuds came then, as the fork was driven viciously, repeatedly down through the straw into the floor.

They're going to find us! They're going to spear us with that thing! Shelly was beginning to panic.

Her fears swirled through her mind. Try as she would she couldn't stop trembling.

Lord, I don't want to die yet. And I'm so scared. I know I belong to you. I gave myself to you and asked you to be my Savior when I was a little girl. I know you love me and are aware of what's happening. Please help Demetri and me get out of here safely.

She sensed a movement near her collar, then Demetri's bare palm was warm against her cheek, comforting her, reminding her that it was imperative that they be silent.

The heavy boots and twanging, thudding pitchfork came closer.

Shelly still couldn't make her legs stop trembling; she barely felt able to breathe, fear tightening her chest like a vice.

Yet, from somewhere deep within her a sense of quiet and peace began to enter her heart.

The crashing, searching pitchfork was closer now, and Shelly could feel the one wielding it must be cursing in anger.

The next plunge of the fork was so close the floor reverberated beneath Shelly's head.

Demetri's hand slid over her mouth, stifling the scream he must have known was rising in her throat.

Through her terror, she heard a shouted mumble of words from another part of the cavernous room.

There was a moment of silence.

Then the pitchfork clattered as it was thrown against the wall.

Footsteps of heavy boots receded.

There were muffled words and short laughter, and finally, the sound of the door slamming.

Shelly's muscles in her arms and legs seemed tied in knots. She ached to be able to move, but she felt Demetri's warm breath against her ear.

"Sh-h. Don't move yet."

He moved his hand from her mouth, but left it against the side of her face.

She watched through the crack as the men appeared from around the barn. She hoped they would go straight to their car, but instead they stopped just outside her hiding place, silhouetted against the stars.

Although she couldn't understand their conversation, she could hear it.

They were so close, Shelly could have reached out and touched their boots had there not been the rough boards of the barn between them.

She heard the crackle of paper, then saw a sudden small flare of light up near the heads of the figures; the aroma of tobacco drifted on the cold air.

Just then something in the straw caused Shelly's nostrils to tingle. She was going to sneeze!

Grabbing her nose with her mittened hand, she tried frantically to hold back the rapidly gathering sneeze.

"Help me, Lord. Please don't let them hear me," her heart breathed to her Heavenly Father.

As though there had been a command, the two men suddenly turned on their heels and headed for the road.

Shelly's sneeze exploded just as someone in the big car started the motor.

They opened the doors and climbed in. Shelly watched relieved as they roared away.

After the taillight had disappeared in the distance, Shelly started to push the straw away from her head.

"No!" Demetri's whisper was like a shot, startling her with its sharpness.

"They talked as though someone might stay behind to watch for any of us who might still be around here somewhere."

More calmly, he continued, "We must stay quiet yet for a while. It is necessary."

Slowly, very carefully, Shelly moved herself into a more comfortable position, pulling from underneath her body her left arm on which she'd fallen. It felt numb and painful, but she was sure it was from the awkward position, not from any injury.

Now that the terror from the intruders had passed, Shelly found herself relaxing a bit, her taut muscles easing.

She didn't feel cold now either. The straw piled around and over her warmed her like a down-filled sleeping bag. The late hour combined with the tension of the past hours were taking their toll, and Shelly drifted off to sleep.

Shelly had no idea how long she may have slept.

She had been deep in a dream . . . *hiding in the drawer of a giant clock. A tiny man wearing boots with turned up toes was standing on the edge of the drawer handing her a small package. The package fell, hitting her on the chin.*

Shelly woke with a start, surrounded by deep silence; Demetri's hand was no longer near her face.

But something was! Something with tiny feet that scurried across her forehead and tried to crawl into her hood.

A mouse! she thought. *Yuk!*

Remembering the danger that might still be present, she moved as quietly as possible, swiping at the intruder with her mittened hand.

The little creature burrowed deeper into her hood. She could feel him at the back of her neck, his tiny feet caught in the mass of hair.

Gritting her teeth to keep from squealing, she cautiously pushed herself to a sitting position. Then with one quick movement she thrust her hood back, and lifted and forced the intruder away with her hand.

Shelly heard a soft movement in the straw and knew the little rodent had scurried away.

Then her thoughts returned to the immediate problem. *Where was Demetri?* she wondered, sensing once again the deep silence in the old building.

She sat listening intently. Hearing no sound, she carefully pushed the straw aside and gazed around into the darkness.

The sound of quiet, hesitating footsteps reached her. She tried to determine their location, then realized someone must be descending the ladder from the loft.

Wondering whether to speak or hide, she decided to remain silent, not moving.

Within moments there were heavy movements in the straw, moving closer and closer to her.

Fear began to clutch at her; something bumped into her.

"Shelly?" A voice whispered.

"Oh, Demetri, it's you!" she whispered back. "Where were you?"

"I went to the loft to get a better view of the surrounding area. I watched for about an hour.

"I feel sure no one is keeping a lookout here anymore. They must have been convinced that everyone had left earlier."

"Can we leave?" Shelly asked.

"Yes, soon," he said, removing a glove and flicking on a tiny flashlight, holding it close to her.

"First, we must check each other and remove any straw clinging to our clothes. Turn around."

Demetri worked quickly, moving the light over her hood, coat and slacks, shielding its glow with his body.

Then he handed it to her and she checked his back where he hadn't been able to.

Pocketing the light she returned to him, he replaced his glove and clasped her hand firmly. "Come."

When Demetri slowly pushed the old door open, it creaked as before. They stood quietly listening before stepping outside.

Darkness was beginning to fade into the grayness that comes just before the hours of dawn. All was silent as Demetri led her diagonally across the field at the back of the barn instead of toward the village.

The snow was deeper here than in the village where it had been cleared or trampled down by many pedestrians.

Shelly found walking difficult even though she lifted her knees as high as possible to maneuver each step through the soft whiteness. She stumbled several times but was steadied by Demetri's firm grip.

They didn't try to talk. Only the sound of their boots crunching through the snow crust, their labored breathing, and the far-off barking of a dog broke the silence.

After a while they arrived at a small road, somewhat protected from the wind by a row of closely spaced spruce trees. Following its path, opened sometime since the last snow by a truck, they came into the village on the far side from where they had left the night before.

They followed a pair of ruts down a snow-covered street until they reached the residential section.

"Does that happen often?" Shelly asked at last. "The interruption at the meeting, I mean."

"Almost every underground church usually experiences it eventually. Especially when the secret police suspect someone may be there whom they're watching."

"Who do they think would be in a church meeting that they'd want?"

"Possibly someone they have warned to stop participating in such activities," Demetri answered. "Sometimes just to harass."

"Well I think it's deplorable."

"It's even beyond deplorable," Demetri said quietly. "And I can understand your shock at the conditions here under which some worship God. I've been shocked myself as I began to learn things."

He paused as they approached an intersecting street. Standing still, he scanned the area. There was no one else in sight.

The wind was rising, becoming even stronger than before. The cold bit into Shelly's face.

"I read, Demetri, that years ago this country was very religious, enough to be known as Holy Russ."

"That is true, Shelly. The Orthodox Church held a lot of influence among the people. But when Communism came into power, the government felt that the Party shouldn't put up with an institution that might have more influence than it did. That's when the persecutions began.

"Many of us began to listen to the wrong people. Those trusting in God became, it seems, a looked-down-upon-minority."

"But why should the government care if the churches had some influence? That should only make living better." Shelly was keeping her voice very low, realizing Demetri was trying to be as unobtrusive as possible.

"You must understand that the philosophy of communism is exactly opposite that of Christianity, Shelly; it is absolutely atheistic.

"Their policy became one of ruthlessness in arresting priests and pastors, exiling many of them. Churches were closed and a campaign of propaganda against all kinds of religious worship began.

"It still continues in one form or another."

"But, Demetri, I've seen documentaries on television that show large churches here with crowds of people in attendance."

"Yes, there are such churches. And I'm sure the Party makes sure that fact is made known."

"They're even put on the itineraries of tourists; it must be true," Shelly insisted.

"But that, too, is something outsiders don't understand," Demetri said, stopping again to scan the next block.

"During the Big War, Stalin wanted to mobilize as many forces as he possibly could, so he gave concessions to the Orthodox Church.

"Because the church has evidently been accountable to secular authority throughout history, it responded well, and the relationship has continued.

"I've learned much in researching many things since I became a working writer."

Demetri suddenly stopped and quickly drew her backward a step into the shadow of a tree.

They had been about to turn a corner to the right into the next block.

"I believe someone is watching your uncle's house," he said quietly. "See that shadow by the second house? His is just across the street."

"It would not be wise for us to go there now. We'll go around another way. I'll take you to my home; my mother will make a place for you to sleep."

They retraced their steps a block and turned in another direction.

"But, Demetri," Shelly protested, "Aunt Tanya and Uncle Vladimer will be worried. They won't know where I am."

"If he arrived home safely, Mr. Rozkalne has undoubtedly noticed the surveillance."

Demetri's mother was praying at the kitchen table when they arrived and greeted them with joy on her thin face.

She bustled around getting tea ready while they removed their outer clothing and boots.

Demetri spoke to her in Russian as the three of them sat at the table enjoying the tea's fragrant warmth. Mrs. Barinov reached over several times to pat Shelly's hand.

When they had finished the hot drinks, she got up from the table, motioning Shelly to follow.

"Good night, Shelly."

"Good night, Demetri," she answered, "or good morning."

Shelly followed Mrs. Barinov through the living room and up a narrow flight of stairs to a large room at the end of a short hall.

While the older woman turned back the covers on one of the two beds and plumped the pillows, Shelly glanced around the simple but cozy room.

A small table with piles of books stacked neatly on its top stood at the side of the lace-curtained window with a chair nearby.

At the end of each bed Shelly saw a small stand with a basin and towel on each; on the floor beneath them, a chamber pot, the only ones she'd ever seen except for those in the historical museum in Gram's town.

Mrs. Barinov closed the drawer of a chest in which she'd been looking and put on Shelly's bed a long gown of some coarse material.

Shelly smiled her thanks, and put her arms around Mrs. Barinov in a gentle hug.

Receiving a hug and pats on her shoulder in return, Shelly felt the words spoken as the woman left were probably, "Sleep well; God bless you."

She recalled passing a phone on the living room wall and wondered if Demetri would call Uncle Vladimer about her being here.

Shelly turned off the small lamp on the table and undressed, putting her clothes on the chair.

Making her way to the bed, she picked up the gown and slipped it over her head, marveling at its softness. She supposed that in spite of its coarse appearance, its texture had evidently been softened through countless washings.

The gown was warm and comforting against her skin as she knelt beside the bed to express her thanksgiving to God for safety that night. And she prayed for Uncle Vladimer and Leonila; she didn't know what had happened to them, either.

Shelly crawled between the covers and was almost instantly asleep.

Chapter Seven

Shelly awoke to sunshine filtering through the curtains and the aroma of frying potatoes drifting through the crack beneath the door.

She found that someone had put a kettle of warm water on the stand, so she quickly bathed and brushed her hair before dressing and making up the bed.

When she went downstairs to the kitchen, Pytor and Galina had already eaten breakfast and left for some part-time work they had in the neighborhood.

Mrs. Barinov put a platter of potatoes and sausage on the table as Shelly entered and Demetri pulled out a chair for her at the table.

"Sleep well?"

"Great," Shelly answered, but instead of sitting down, she said to him, "I appreciate your family's hospitality, but I think I ought to get to Aunt Tanya's as soon as possible to let them know I'm okay and to see if they are."

"Eat with us, Shelly," he coaxed. "I'll try again to reach them by phone. Our service is not always dependable out here, and I couldn't contact them early this morning."

Shelly sat down, and by the time Mrs. Barinov had placed bread and tea on the table, he was back from the other room.

Smiling, he said, "I spoke to Mrs. Rozkalne and told her you were having breakfast with us.

"Vladimer and Leonila were able to slip out a small side door last night and hurried away while the police were in the barn and chasing others."

"I'm so thankful they're all right. Thank you for taking care of me, Demetri. I don't know what foolish thing I might have done if you hadn't been with me."

Mrs. Barinov had gone into an adjoining room, so while they

were eating, Shelly resumed an earlier conversation.

"You were telling me a bit about the Orthodox Church. What about the other churches? Why are they persecuted and why so many restrictions? Uncle Vladimer told me about the registration."

"It's all part of the demand to follow Communist doctrine, Shelly. The restrictions are to try to bring the Christians in line, so to speak.

"For instance, in order for a clergyman to serve as pastor of a specific church, he must be cleared by the Council for Religious Affairs. This is a government agency and it's common knowledge that it is run mainly by the KGB. Also, the government has control over whether a church can repair its building, or even use a particular building."

"Then being registered doesn't necessarily prevent a church from having problems, does it?" Shelly asked.

"No, it doesn't. In fact, a friend of mine told me of his cousin, soon to graduate from the Orthodox seminary, who had been approached by a KGB man and asked to spy on his associates."

Shelly shook her head slowly, "It's very difficult to realize that situations like this really exist. How sad that your government doesn't acknowledge God."

"Yes, Shelly, it is tragic for many because they never get to know the Lord. Yet in spite of the indoctrination in atheism from the time we start school, some of the citizens do find Him."

"But how can they unless they're reared in a Christian home or are attending a church?"

"I'll show you an example," Demetri answered, getting up and bringing an envelope from a small wood box on a table just inside the living room.

"This arrived just two days ago from my mother's girlhood friend in an isolated Siberian village.

"They heard a Christian radio broadcast; the very first time they had heard of Jesus Christ.

"They began listening consistently and also told their friends about the programs they had discovered.

"Soon a number of them had given their lives to the Lord. Since there was no church in their area, they began gathering in one or another of the new Christian's homes at the times of the Gospel broadcasts.

"The preacher speaking to them over the radio waves became, in effect, their pastor. So, now they are a church, although not in ways you are probably accustomed to."

"That's wonderful, Demetri," Shelly responded.

Demetri smiled, "I've learned the past few years that God is working in many ways to reveal himself to the people willing to listen."

Demetri stood up and went for Shelly's coat, "Now I must see that you get safely to your uncle's home."

Aunt Tanya greeted them at the door when they arrived. She had her coat on and was stepping into her boots. "This is one of my days to work," she said. "I must leave now so I don't miss my train.

"I'll see you this evening, Shelly," she added, giving her a hug. "Leonila is upstairs."

"I'll be going, too," Demetri said, giving Shelly's hand a gentle pressure. "I will be in Moscow for a few days preparing for some upcoming articles. I'll contact you when I return."

When they had left, Shelly went to the bottom of the stairs, "Leonila?"

"Yes, Shelly. In a moment I will be down," she answered.

Ivan and little Anna clattered down the stairs after her to smile shyly at Shelly.

Leonila bent over to whisper something to them, followed by a loud "Sh-h" as they ran back up the stairs.

"It is good to see you are all right, Shelly. I was afraid for you last night. I just now told the children they must play very quietly because it's to be a secret that we are visiting here."

"What do you think will happen if the authorities do discover you're here?" Shelly asked. "Do you really think they would cause trouble for Uncle Vladimer?"

"Because of their threats, it can be expected. But," she added, tears in her eyes, "I have nowhere else to go. I have no relatives in this area."

Shelly put her arm around Leonila, "Uncle Vladimer told me your home had been confiscated. Didn't they leave anything for you?"

"Just our clothing and a trunk to keep them in. Also a box of kitchen utensils."

Then she smiled, "They did permit me to take the children's toys. I was happy for that because Fyodor had carved them for Anna and Ivan."

"Did they let you have your husband's clothing?"

"They said I could not have them, but while the authorities were not watching me I packed some of them anyway, under the children's things and under the kitchen dishes and pots and pans.

"They made me shove the box out on the porch by the trunk. Then they locked the doors and left us there."

"What an awful thing for them to do," Shelly said. "How mean to treat little children that way."

"Yes," Leonila said, starting to prepare some tea, "but I am thankful they left the children with me. We have heard of others whose children were taken and placed in a state school. They do not see them again."

Shelly sat wide-eyed. "Christians here face much more than I had ever imagined, and there's nothing I can do to help any of you."

"There is something you can do, Shelly. I was going to ask you if you wanted to assist me."

"What is it?" Shelly asked. "I'll be glad to help you."

"Do you have a Bible or New Testament with you?"

"I have a Testament."

"Is good," Leonila said, bringing an apron-wrapped package from the far side of the table.

Opening it, she picked up a large book with a very worn cover. Beneath it was a stack of blank paper.

"When the police took my Fyodor and the two girls, they also confiscated every Bible in the church. We had this one at home in the old trunk; it belonged to Fyodor's grandmother.

"Also, the Barinovs were able to hide theirs and it wasn't taken. The church has been using it in the secret meeting. A Christian neighbor of theirs always walks to the meetings with Mrs. Barinov to protect it when her son-in-law, Pytor, doesn't attend.

"I have been making handwritten copies of some of the new Testament books and Psalms," Leonila added, spreading the things out on the table.

"Mrs. Barinov gave me paper to use that had been stored in an attic cubbyhole at the house when her son, Pavel, was arrested for printing Bible study guides and literature for the children.

"Pavel always kept an extra supply there, anticipating possible trouble. Even in difficult times, we have seen in various ways how our God has helped us prepare ahead for our needs now."

"And you want me to do some copying, too?" Shelly asked.

"Yes."

"I'll do my best at copying, Leonila, but I'm not familiar with writing your alphabet, or printing it."

Leonila laughed lightly, "No, no, Shelly. Your own Testament you can use. You can copy quickly from it and we will share those copies with the folks who can read English."

Shelly's face brightened, her smile expressing her relief.

"Then we will sew them into little books," Leonila added, "each one containing a Gospel or several groups of Psalms."

"I'll run upstairs and get my Testament," Shelly said.

When she returned, Leonila was bringing tea to the table. "Tanya said a birthday party is being planned for next week."

"Whose birthday?" Shelly asked.

"Vladimer's."

"But his birthday was in June," Shelly said. "I remember sending a card to him."

"Yes, Shelly, you are correct. But this is a special party. Tanya said she heard about this type of celebration from a friend at work who lives in Salyak.

"This lady, also, is a member of an unregistered church. Because it is usual for families and friends to gather for someone's birthday, the church uses these occasions for meetings. It is a safe way to be in a group; the worshipers can sing loudly without worry.

"If the get-together is questioned, they're having a birthday."

"That woman in Salyak said some of the members there have several birthdays each year. It makes opportunity for fairly regular extra meetings where they need not be fearful of detection. A party is accepted as commonplace by any observer."

"It sounds as though people wanting to worship together have learned to improvise. There's an old saying in America that where there's a will, there's a way."

Leonila smiled, "Is true. The Salyak people also include extra preaching and singing in funeral services, even weddings. The pastor is asked at the party to come up and congratulate the bride and groom so he can speak to the group about the Lord."

"I admire the Christians here," Shelly said. "They don't seem to feel helpless, nor do they give up because of these difficulties."

"Some do," Leonila said, "because of extra pressures and threats to their families. I am frightened myself."

"You have every right to be," Shelly said. "I think you're doing very well under the circumstances."

Shelly and Leonila spent most of the day copying Scriptures in the smallest legible script they could on the sheets they had cut to an easily concealed size.

When Uncle Vladimer and Aunt Tanya returned home that evening, supper was prepared and waiting.

The young women had put aside their work, and the delicious aroma of spiced cabbage mingled with that of sausages and potatoes as pan lids were removed and food dished into bowls.

The kitchen was warm and cozy, protected from the intense cold outside that swirled in when the door was opened.

Ivan and Anna, fresh from naps, were already seated at the table, their round little faces wreathed in smiles as they greeted Vladimer and Tanya.

Conversation around the table that evening centered on Valentina, with everyone excited and hopeful about the possibility of her release.

"Can you find out whether she'll be released ahead of time as her friend was?" Shelly asked.

"Perhaps," Uncle Vladimer answered. "I go to Garonkuk Prison tomorrow after work. Tomorrow I work half day."

"Maybe she can come back with him," Aunt Tanya said.

"We will hope," Uncle Vladimer responded, "but whatever our God permits, we will accept without complaining." He reached over to pat his wife's hand.

"I hope, also," Aunt Tanya stated, nodding toward the door to great-aunt Natalia's room, "that Mamma is stronger tomorrow and can join the fellowship around the table. She has been eating so little."

Fixing a small plate of food and setting a glass of tea on a tray, she started for the door.

"Let me, Aunt Tanya," Shelly said, reaching for the tray. "We get along fine together, Aunt Natalia and I."

But Aunt Natalia was sleeping when Shelly went in with her supper. The frail little woman appeared to be even weaker than earlier that day.

Gently waking her, Shelly helped her freshen up a bit and then fed her some supper. Aunt Natalia ate little, seeming to have no appetite, trying only to please Shelly. But she did enjoy the tea, sipping it bit by bit as Shelly helped her hold the warm glass.

By the time Shelly had replaced the glass on the tray, Aunt Natalia was already asleep. Shelly tucked the covers around her thin shoulders and tiptoed back to the kitchen.

Aunt Tanya looked at the food left on the plate and shook her head sadly.

"She's sleeping already," Shelly said.

Uncle Vladimer wiped the corner of his eye, "Soon, I think, she will be resting where our Lord is."

Then turning to little Anna, he smiled broadly, "Come, Anna, little Dochka." Lifting her onto his lap, he began softly singing a song while he played a finger game with her and Ivan.

Aunt Tanya said to Shelly, "Tomorrow I go for milk for the children. Would you like to go with me?"

Shelly nodded.

"Perhaps, too," Aunt Tanya continued, "we can find some good tvorog to celebrate Valentina's homecoming. It is her favorite cheese."

A sense of happy expectancy began to pervade the room, growing as the evening progressed, enhanced by a time of prayer together when they joined hands around the table before the children's bedtime.

Later as Shelly lay on her own bed, her heart became heavy with thoughts of the problems faced by the individuals under this roof.

Then thinking about Demetri, she realized how much she would miss him when she left the Soviet Union.

The morning was bright and clear, but the air was bitingly cold as Shelly and Aunt Tanya, both carrying string shopping bags, walked to the area of small shops.

Although it was still quite early, lines were already forming, housewives and older men purchasing the day's bread and milk, hoping to find something extra finally in stock.

As they stood in one of the lines, Shelly said, "Aunt Tanya, you wouldn't let me contribute anything toward the food expenses when I spoke to you about it, but I'd very much like to."

"You are our guest, Shelly; it would not do."

"Then will you at least let me get something special for Valentina's homecoming supper?"

Aunt Tanya hesitated; then a smile brightened her face, "For that, Shelly, yes. Some canned salmon, perhaps. We all would enjoy that with some of my pickles and the tvorog for our zakuski."

"Zakuski?" Shelly questioned.

"I am sorry; how to say in English?" Aunt Tanya smiled. "Ah, appetizers; the little special bits that add much to the pleasure of a celebration meal."

"How about some fresh fruit for dessert?" Shelly asked.

"Nyet, never in the winter is it available to us here in the village. Only apples occasionally. But I thank you for offering, Shelly."

When they returned home, Leonila was at the table diligently copying from the Gospel of John.

"A good idea that copying is, Leonila," Aunt Tanya said. "How far along are you?"

"This is the third one since they took Fyodor away. Only the New Testament books with a few psalms I am working on. Two I have finished and sewn together, but I had nothing to make covers."

"Ach, yes, that would be a help in protecting them. We will have to think of something to use."

Aunt Tanya removed the bread, then put her net-bag containing the cheese and milk outside the door.

"Gram told me once about keeping perishables that way," Shelly said, sitting at the far end of the table across from Leonila, getting ready to continue her copying.

"You know," she said, "I have two new pair of jeans in my suitcase. The fabric is very strong and would make suitable covers, I think, Leonila. And since you want the booklets easily concealed, they would be very flexible."

"Oh, Shelly, perfect that would be," Leonila said, looking up with a smile. Then she stopped, looking a bit sheepish. "But your clothing; I would not want to ask that."

"I want to do it," Shelly said. "I can get along without them. We'll cut pieces to fit the little pages tonight."

Aunt Tanya looked at her with eyebrows raised, "Shelly doesn't know what her jeans are worth here; that many times the American cost she could get on nalevo."

"Nalevo?" Shelly questioned.

"What you would call the black market, I think, Shelly," Leonila explained. "Or sometimes it is a sort of bartering that goes on for wanted items, especially in the cities, because many things are very scarce."

"Well, nalevo or not," Shelly said, laughing lightly, "we'll use my jeans, if they're suitable, to cover God's Word. Gram wanted me to help here if there was any way that I could. Contributing my jeans is a small thing."

During the rest of the day, the two young women could sense Aunt Tanya's anticipation of Uncle Vladimer's return, and her longing that Valentina might be returning with him.

It was early dusk when they heard him scraping and stomping snow from his boots.

Aunt Tanya hurried to the door and flung it open.

Uncle Vladimer came in, his shoulders stooping, shaking his head.

"They would not release her," he said dejectedly. "I pleaded with them. It was unlike me, but I even tried to bribe them and almost got arrested myself. But she is my Valentina, my only little girl." Tears slid down his cheeks into his wide mustache.

"But why?" Aunt Tanya cried. "Why was Olga freed and our Valentina not?"

"For an infraction of the rules, they said, Valentina must stay two more months."

"What did she do?" Tears were running down Aunt Tanya's cheeks now, too. "What, that would make necessary a two-month jail sentence extra? She is a good girl."

"For refusing to stop spreading anti-Soviet propaganda, they told me."

Uncle Vladimer sank heavily into a chair by the table, not even removing his coat and hat or heavy boots. As he sat, the snow melted into a puddle around his feet, out on the rug beneath the table.

"Only a few minutes they gave me with her. She said she would talk only of God. To one of the other inmates she spoke telling of His love, His death for them. Our dear, brave Valentina. Our little girl . . ."

His voice broke as he turned his face toward the wall to hide his tears.

Chapter Eight

Supper that night was not the festive affair they had planned. The women didn't even bother to open the canned salmon or the container of tvorog, but left them in the storage bag. "Valentina will be freed soon," Aunt Tanya said in a brave attempt to encourage the others. "We will enjoy the special foods when she is here with us."

After Leonila and Shelly had tucked the youngsters into bed and were sitting on Shelly's bed talking, Leonila said, "I have been asking the heavenly Father to let something happen so Fyodor will be freed.

"The children and I miss him and I know I am asking for myself, but the church here needs him also."

"I'll pray for his release, too," Shelly assured her as she reached over to squeeze Leonila's hand.

Shelly fell asleep wondering how she would bear the strain if Demetri were her husband and in the situation Leonila's Fyodor was.

Two evenings later, Demetri arrived with a request for Uncle Vladimer and Shelly.

"My mother has finally heard from my brother, Pavel. He is being held at Kresty Prison in Leningrad. He says we will be allowed to visit and bring food and clothing.

"He thinks he will be also permitted to reopen his print shop when he's home again."

"Oh, I am so happy for your mother," Aunt Tanya said. "How happy she must be to finally know his whereabouts."

"Yes, a great joy it was for all of us," Demetri said. "But she is not feeling well enough for the trip. Galina and Pytor both feel they must not miss the bit of work they've been able to obtain, so

I wondered if Shelly might be permitted to go to Leningrad with me?"

Turning to Uncle Vladimer, he continued, "Visitors from other countries usually visit the Hermitage when in Leningrad area, so I thought she might enjoy some sightseeing, too."

Vladimer nodded his approval.

"Would you like to accompany me, Shelly?" Demetri asked.

"Yes, I would," she answered, her eyes sparkling.

"Good. Being able to show you some of the beauty of Leningrad will make the sadness of seeing my brother in prison easier to bear.

"Pavel will be there for at least two months," he said, turning to the Rozkalnes. "The address of the prison is Sledstvennyi Izolyator, 45/1, if you want to write to him. They told him he could receive letters and have two visitors."

Heading for the door, Demetri said to Shelly, "We must leave very early in the morning, on the first train. I will be here for you at four-thirty."

The commuter train moved swiftly across the frozen landscape in the early morning darkness, stopping occasionally in villages along the way to pick up passengers.

Shelly watched with interest the men in rough workclothes or dressier topcoats, and women wearing babushkas tied closely around their heads against the penetrating cold.

"Galina showed me a photograph of Pavel and her taken just the week before his arrest," Shelly said as a young couple sat down across from them.

"They both resemble your mother, I think. Do you have your father's features?"

"Mother always said so," Demetri answered, smiling. "I wish you could have known him; he was a kind man. His death several years ago, shortly after Pavel's arrest, hurt her deeply."

When the train deposited them at a station in the city, they walked immediately to the street corner where a large group was waiting for continuing transportation.

The icy sidewalk was covered with new snow, and white frost covered the streetcar cables and the branches of several stunted trees.

Demetri said, "We will hope there is not a long wait for a tram. I am sure you are not used to this type of dense cold."

"It gets quite cold in Chicago, too, Demetri," Shelly laughed. "You might be surprised at some of our winters, though I must confess it's not usually *this* cold, at least not for extended periods."

Several streetcars came by, one clanking and screeching as it came to a stop to take on some of the heavily bundled people waiting stolidly around Shelly and Demetri in the frigid air.

Snow began falling in soft swirls again as the next car approached. Demetri raised his arm to hail the tram, and the two got on.

"This is such an old and lovely city," Shelly said, her gaze shifting quickly as they moved with a swaying smoothness over the glistening whiteness.

The tram slowed as they crossed an impressive bridge, and Shelly pressed her forehead against the window to look at the expanse of frozen water below.

"That's the Neva River," Demetri said. "It has three main branches throughout the city."

"Have you been here often?" Shelly asked.

"The university is here," Demetri answered. "This is, as you say, my alma mater city."

"I thought we would ride to the promenade along the main Neva and since the snow has stopped, perhaps we might take a short stroll." He looked at her questioningly with a winsome grin.

"I think I'd like that, Demetri. That is, if I don't freeze."

"We won't let that happen," he said, laughing. "We'll go just a short way if you get too cold."

"Leningrad certainly has a lot of impressive buildings," Shelly remarked, her gaze following them as they passed. "Can you tell me what some of them are?"

"That is the State Public Library, filled with many, many volumes. It was once the Imperial Library.

"Ah," he said pointing, "that great building there with the semicircular colonnade of Corinthian columns, the Cathedral of Our Lady of Kozan."

"It's lovely," Shelly said.

The tram stopped now to dispense and take up passengers.

"What is that golden-spired building way ahead of us that looks almost like it centers the street?"

"The Admiralty, Shelly. This principal thoroughfare and the two others of Leningrad meet there in the center of the city."

He smiled at her, appreciating her enjoyment. "When we arrive there you will see at the Admiralty's southwest corner a beautiful building, once the Cathedral of St. Isaac. It, like many others, is no longer a place of worship, but is used as a museum.''

"Yes," Shelly said softly, "I've read about that."

They left the tram near the Admiralty and crossed the icy street to a stone parapet overlooking the Neva River from which an embankment sloped to the water's edge.

"Fishing is good along here in the summer," Demetri stated as they looked down at the immobile, ice-blocked river. Frozen vapor rose from its surface and drifted along the snow-covered ground.

They turned then and walked together down the almost-deserted promenade. Demetri offered her his arm, and she tucked her hand into the crook of his elbow. They walked in silence for a few moments, then Demetri stopped and pointed toward the river.

"Shelly, look over there. You'll see Voselevski Island. That building nearest us is the Academy of Arts with its museum. The other one that you can easily see is the University of Leningrad.''

"Where you studied?"

"Yes."

"Is it very expensive to attend the university?"

"Here those who get into the university have their education subsidized."

"It must be very difficult to gain entrance."

"Yes, for some," Demetri said. "For others, not too difficult.''

Sensing he wanted to change the subject, Shelly asked, "Are there other islands in the river that are utilized as much as that one?"

"Yes," Demetri answered. "One that might be of interest to you is a small one on which is a little wood house. It is where Peter the Great lived when he started to build St. Petersburg, which most now call Leningrad."

"That *is* interesting, Demetri. Sort of like the log cabins we have in America from the time of the settlers."

"That is so," Demetri returned.

"This river area contains a lot of things important to your country's history, doesn't it?"

"Yes it does, Shelly."

Demetri turned her to face him. "There are two very important things concerning both our histories that I want to talk with you about, also."

"Our histories?" Shelly's look was puzzled, but something in

Demetri's eyes stirred an excitement within her.

He nodded solemnly, "But that we will talk about later. You are getting cold, are you not? Your nose looks like a cherry, a very pretty one, I might add," he teased with a grin.

Shelly giggled. "Yours doesn't look sculptured in ivory, either."

"In that case, we both would benefit from a warm spot, would we not? Come."

"Where are we going?" Shelly asked.

"You would perhaps like to do a bit of shopping?"

"Oh, yes, I would like to take a few things to Aunt Tanya and perhaps Leonila's children."

"Good," Demetri said, "we shall hope to find what you want, often one cannot. Then we will have an early lunch."

Later as they sat in the restaurant enjoying a thick soup following their herrings and salad, Shelly asked, "What did you want to tell me about our histories?"

Very slowly Demetri took a sip of tea.

"Concerning what I am going to say, perhaps to ask you, I expect no answer now. But tell you, I must."

Then he sat silent, looking at her, his eyes darkening with feeling, his gaze gentle, yet intense with an emotion that caused her heart to beat quickly.

When she felt she couldn't stand the waiting any longer, she said, "Yes, Demetri?"

He took a deep breath, then reaching across the table, he put his large hand over her small one.

"Shelly, I love you. Something very strong began growing in my heart from the first time I saw you on the train.

"It shook me deeply. I tried to convince myself while I was away in Moscow that it was just an infatuation."

Shelly sat quietly, her own blossoming love for him barely concealed.

Demetri continued, "I have been struggling with this and praying much about it. And I know with absolute certainty that it is so."

He moved his hand back across the table and absently picked up his knife, looking at it.

"It is an impossible thing. There is such disparity in our backgrounds, and our countries have opposing ideologies. It is almost as though we are from different times. We are so unlike each other."

He shook his head dejectedly, "Like a knife it is to my heart."

It was Shelly who reached across the table this time, her fingertips touching his hand. "We are not so different, Demetri," she said softly.

"We both love the Lord and belong to Him. We are equals in His sight. Where we came into the world, or our educations, these aren't the most important things."

"Yes, deep in my heart I know that, Shelly," he said, putting down the knife and turning his hand to enfold hers.

"But the prospect of our being together is all but impossible. The obstacles seem insurmountable, right now at least."

"I know, Demetri," Shelly said very softly. "But if our God has planned it, it will happen in His time. You told me yourself the day we met that nothing God plans surprises you. Remember?"

Very gently he smiled. "You are younger than I, Shelly, yet you have to remind me of that which I should have uppermost in my heart and mind."

They were both silent as they finished their bowls of soup and ate the delicious halva and ice cream.

When they left the restaurant, Demetri said, "We are not far from the Hermitage, and the Winter Palace.

"We won't have time to see both. Perhaps I can tell you about the Winter Palace and we'll go to the Hermitage. It is one of the leading art galleries in the world."

As they walked along the snowy iced sidewalk, Shelly's heart was soaring with the revelation of Demetri's love.

His voice broke her reverie, "The Winter Palace also has much artwork. It was the official residence of the Czar until 1917 when he abdicated.

"It has an enormous amount of rooms, all decorated with many valuable paintings and sculptures. It is said that when all the apartments were occupied, the palace held 6500 people."

"Wow, I'd hate to have to cook or make beds for that many guests," Shelly mused. Then with a giggle, she added, "Do you know you sound just like a tour guide?"

Demetri chuckled, "Well, you said I could tell you about it and so I am doing."

Shelly smiled, her mittened hand lightly squeezing Demetri's arm through his heavy coat.

"So now, on to the Hermitage," he said, guiding her carefully across an especially slippery spot.

"Which, incidentally," he added with a sideways grin, "is made up of the Imperial Palace and three other buildings, known as the State Hermitage Museum." He ended with an exaggerated flourish, almost causing them both to lose their footing.

They stood laughing, arms around each other, eyes sparkling.

Noticing that they were being appreciatively watched by passersby, they quickly composed themselves into more dignified demeanors.

Approaching a park, Shelly saw at the entrance two elderly women, bundled against the cold, sitting chatting.

"It surely doesn't seem like a decent day for sitting in a park," she said, inclining her head toward them.

"It's not exactly by choice, Shelly. They are dezhurnayas; duty-women guarding the park gates. It is their job. Many of them there are, in the cities especially."

"But why would a park gate need guarding?"

Demetri paused, "It is something that is done here," he said quietly. "Always, everything is observed, and reported."

Walking past the entrance, Demetri nodded pleasantly to the two women, and Shelly smiled and waved.

Through the iron fence she could see a large ice rink where a group of children of varying ages were being instructed in skating.

Shelly smiled as a tiny tot slipped and rolled like a fur ball in his heavy clothes.

Beyond the park she saw an old church and marveled at the size of the stone edifice and its onion-topped towers. The onion-points held aloft crosses shining white in the sun that had come out from behind the clouds.

As they approached the area surrounding the Winter Palace, Shelly saw a large group of women, each one wrapped round and round by a large black shawl, sweeping the walks and entrance expanse clean of new-fallen snow. Their crude brooms were swinging rhythmically as though they were scything grain.

Loaded buses lined the street approaching the Hermitage, and a line of people was entering the building.

Elderly women manning the coat rooms took coats, scarves, gloves, and overshoes.

Taking their turn, Demetri and Shelly sidestepped the cleaning women bent over the foyer floor, mopping up the melting snow being tracked in.

Shelly and Demetri spent the rest of the morning enjoying the excellent collections of priceless paintings and Greek and Roman sculptures. Shelly was caught up in the wonder of works like Leonardo's *Madonna*, and Rembrandt's *Prodigal Son*, and could have stayed for hours, but Demetri reminded her it was time to go.

They boarded a bus for the other side of the city, and as they settled into a seat, Demetri slipped his arm around Shelly and pulled her closer to him. She relaxed her head against his strong chest, feeling safe in his love and protection.

The dangers of the past weeks seem to fade in her memory. Perhaps this country wasn't such a terrible place after all. If only the security and joy of this moment could stretch on forever.

But Demetri's voice broke into her complacent daydream, and jerked her back into the painful realities still around them.

"Come, Shelly," he said. "The prison is ahead . . ."

Chapter Nine

The bus had stopped now and people were alighting.

When they were standing on the slippery ground and the bus had passed, Shelly saw a large building across the street and she wondered if Pavel could be inside. She felt relieved that it looked rather nice.

But instead Demetri turned her to face the opposite direction, and led her to a street leading off along the river at a right angle from where the bus had left them.

They started down the street marked *Arsenal'naya Quay*, approaching a massive stone wall on their left that seemed to run for a long distance.

"Is this the prison?" Shelly asked. "I noticed an extension of this wall along the street we just left."

"Yes, it is, Shelly. The complex in there houses at least ten thousand prisoners; also a psychiatric hospital."

"So many imprisoned people," Shelly said, surprised. "Are most of them actually criminals?"

"Many are, of course," Demetri answered. "But most of them? Perhaps not; who can know?"

Ahead of them several people who had gotten off the bus when they did were turning to go through an entrance into the forbidding looking wall.

Demetri guided Shelly through after them. "This is the location for waiting to leave a parcel for a prisoner," he explained. "Pavel sent the instructions."

They entered a small oblong courtyard where a crowd had formed. Soft snowflakes drifted onto fur collars and threadbare coats alike. Warm fur hats and cloth babushkas acquired the same whiteness. Status made no difference; all were alike in the waiting.

Expensive polished leather boots and cloth-wrapped feet in old overshoes both made footprints of persons with sad hearts hoping for a glimpse of a loved one.

Shelly saw that everyone there carried filled string bags or parcels. One by one, the figures moved through the snow to a window in an inner wall and left their parcels.

"Most look so forlorn," Shelly said.

"It is no wonder; they are evidently not being permitted to go in."

After standing, with heads down dejectedly for several minutes as though undecided what to do, one family passed from Shelly's view back through the high stone wall. The spaces they vacated were soon filled by others arriving, moving slowly forward in the lines.

"It seems to take forever, doesn't it, Demetri?" Shelly said as the line they were in hardly seemed to move.

"Yes, but we are used to lines in my country—lines to see what the store has in stock, lines to pay, lines to pick up the items."

Eventually, they stood before the window.

Instead of handing in the parcels as the others had, Demetri seemed to be insisting on something.

The only thing Shelly could understand was the "nyet! nyet!" repeated by the uniformed man inside the room.

Then with a determined look, Demetri took his wallet from an inner pocket and flipped it open under the guard's face, saying something to him very quietly.

The man looked up with a startled glance, hesitated a moment, then picked up a phone.

After a short conversation, he hung up and nodded curtly to Demetri.

Another guard opened a door and led them through the package receiving room to a small anteroom.

Soon two other guards appeared, their uniforms with the red collar tabs and black belts dusted with snow.

They escorted Shelly and Demetri across an open area enclosed by a massive wall, toward a foreboding building.

One of the guards held his automatic weapon ready as they crossed an expanse where a group of prisoners were sweeping snow away from a building's entrance under the watchful eye of a guard.

Shelly's gaze strayed up the side of the tall building and over its boarded-up cell windows. She wondered who was behind each one, and why.

"Look, Demetri," she said, pointing upward as they rounded the corner of the immense structure. "Look up there. Only one of the windows on those two sides is unobstructed, and it has a clean glass pane. Why do you suppose it's different from the others?"

He spoke briefly with the guards then said, "That's the cell where Lenin was imprisoned at one time. Evidently conditions have changed a lot since those days.

"They said Lenin had the cell to himself and had the window through which he could see the sunshine and the sky. They have kept it the same as then in his memory, I guess."

"What about all those covered windows? No one could possibly see the sky or anything else through them."

"I don't know, Shelly. They said those windows have always been muzzled as long as they've been working here."

"Are we on our way to see Pavel?" Shelly asked.

"The prison commander, Colonel Smirnov," Demetri answered.

They were escorted through a guarded entrance of the harsh-looking building and into an office where a cold-eyed man behind a desk arrogantly looked them over.

A sentence to him by Demetri brought forth the familiar "nyet."

Then Demetri spoke again. This time the middle-aged, greying man looked over at Shelly, and hesitated a moment. Then he rose from his chair and bowed his head toward Shelly in a show of courtesy.

With an obviously false smile of welcome, he said, "Ah, from America, once our ally in the Great War of Freedom from the evil Hitler.

"You are enjoying your visit in our great Soviet Union?"

"Thank you," Shelly answered. "It has been very enlightening."

"Da, Da. And also you shall see our great compassion even for those who have acted against our government. We will let one of the disturbed ones have visit by his brother, this fine comrade here."

He leaned forward, both hands on his desk, "And you, too; you shall accompany him, yes? You shall see how well the deluded ones are cared for in our great land."

Shelly glanced quickly at Demetri, catching his slight nod.

"Yes, thank you very much," she said, giving Colonel Smirnov a smile, thankful that she wouldn't have to stay in this dreary room with this man while Demetri visited Pavel.

She and Demetri followed the uniformed man who escorted them from the room to a flight of stairs leading downward. Shelly was very conscious that another guard was behind them, his hand on his weapon.

"Do you think they're going to take us into Pavel's cell?" she asked Demetri.

"I doubt it. Unless I'm confused about the direction, I believe this long hallway we are entering may be the tunnel under the river that leads to the KGB administration building and their prison complex. You may have noticed that large imposing building we passed just before the bus crossed the bridge."

Shelly had seen the building, and the thought of entering it now was unnerving.

Soon they entered another corridor, this one wide and carpeted.

They were motioned into a small room, bare except for several chairs. Removing their coats, they sat down to wait.

The guards stationed themselves just outside the doorway.

"I was told I'm to have ten minutes with him," Demetri said.

They hadn't heard the footsteps in the carpeted hall, but after an hour's wait, another pair of guards appeared, shoved a man into the room and joined their peers outside the doorway.

"Pavel?" Demetri asked the forlorn, stooped figure.

The gaunt man's head raised, the frightened eyes focused warily on Demetri for a few seconds.

"Pavel? It's Demetri," he said, rising and moving forward.

A glint of recognition appeared in the glazed eyes. Weakly he raised a hand toward Demetri.

Shelly's eyes filled with tears as Demetri strode across the space and enveloped the thin figure in his arms.

Tears were streaming from the eyes of both men, and Pavel's frail shoulders shook with sobs.

Surely this old man can't be Pavel, Shelly thought. *Not the handsome, young Pavel I saw in the photo*. Yet, she knew from Demetri's actions that it was Pavel.

Demetri led the shuffling, haggard man over to where Shelly sat. She rose as he said, "Pavel, this is Shelly Lee, a friend from America, a relative of the Rozkalnes' in Orensk."

A small, sincere smile started first in Pavel's eyes, then moved to his trembling lips as they tried to form an extension of the greeting.

He held out his hand and when she took it, his eyes seemed to clear a bit as they searched hers carefully.

"God is with you, Pavel," she said, enclosing his hand in both of hers. "Know that I will be praying for you."

Pavel's tears began flowing again, and he looked beseechingly toward Demetri.

"Yes, Pavel, I, too, love God now. I know Jesus died for me and have asked Him to come into my heart."

"I thank God," Pavel said, pulling his hand from Shelly's gentle grasp and grabbing his brother's arms. "Thank God," he repeated, rejoicing. "Many years I have prayed for this."

Then he glanced fearfully toward the guards lounging in the hall. But they seemed oblivious, either not understanding English or not caring about the conversation.

"Our family is well, Pavel," Demetri said, his arm around his brother, guiding him to a chair between his and Shelly's.

"Our Father is with the Lord. He died shortly after your arrest."

Pavel appeared stunned, but only nodded his head, saying nothing.

A moment later, Shelly heard his voice, very low. "He is well off. I am glad. Better that. He might otherwise have also come to this."

While Demetri mentioned other family members and friends, Shelly's hand slipped from her pocket unobtrusively into Pavel's.

"How have they been treating you, Pavel?" Demetri asked.

His answer was a short, harsh laugh. Then, glancing again toward the door before speaking, he said, "For two years I was in hard-labor camp, without first even a trial.

"Since they have brought me here, they try to make me sign confession to activities against the government."

Pavel's dulled eyes flashed a small spark of determination. "I refused. Three separate times I have spent in solitary cell too small to sit down in. Cold it was there, so cold."

Demetri slipped his arm around his brother's thin stooped shoulders as Pavel continued. "In this mental hospital I have been for how long I am not sure. They force injections on me.

"I do not know how long my mind can resist the drugs. Perhaps I shall sign without even knowing."

Slowly Pavel shook his head, then lifted his chin with a slight smile. "These doctors tell me that surely I am insane to believe there is a God and to waste materials printing such trashy propaganda when my print shop was needed for important community things."

Shelly shivered inwardly, thankful that she lived in a country where she wouldn't be subjected to such treatment.

Little did she suspect what was ahead of her.

One of the guards appeared in the doorway, pointing to his watch, and though Shelly couldn't understand his words, the implication was clear.

The three of them stood as the two guards who had brought Pavel in approached.

Quickly Demetri embraced Pavel, then gave him the parcels.

Clasping them against his chest, Pavel was grabbed by his upper arms by the men and hustled out of the room.

Shelly and Demetri put their coats on and followed the remaining guards who were beckoning.

After they were escorted back through the corridors, out of the building and across the large courtyard, they were taken into the small courtyard next to the parcel room, where they had to push their way through the waiting crowd, lined up patiently in the falling snow.

As they passed through the massive outer wall of the prison complex and emerged onto the sidewalk along Arsenal'naya Quay, Shelly said, "I'm glad you were able to see that Pavel actually got the packages you brought."

"Yes, I, too," Demetri said. "Whether or not they let him keep them is another matter."

"You think they may not?" Shelly asked.

"It is possible. We hear it often happens."

"Well, I surely hope it doesn't happen this time," she said.

Just before they turned to head for the tram corner, they saw in the opposite direction a dark van stop along the oppressive wall, turn and disappear through an entrance beyond the one from which they had just exited.

Shelly shuddered, visualizing the prisoners huddled inside.

Both were silent during the bus ride back to the train station, the image of Pavel's gaunt and broken figure weighing heavily on their minds.

It seemed so hopeless to Shelly. The Communist Party was so cruel, so unjust. What hope did Demetri see for Pavel?

Suddenly her mind flashed back to her conversation with Demetri at lunch. He had said then he had two important things to tell her, but the second thing had gotten lost in the excitement of his admission of his love for her.

"Demetri?"

Her voice roused him from his thoughts, and he gave his head a slight shake, as if to clear away the gloom of the scene they'd just witnessed.

"Yes, Shelly?"

"Demetri, earlier today you said you had two important things to tell me, but we didn't seem to make it past the first announcement." A blush made her cheeks glow, and he smiled down at her.

"What else did you want to say?"

Suddenly Demetri's smile faded, and he looked away. His lips became a tight line, and he was silent.

The sudden change in his expression caught Shelly off guard.

"Shelly," he said slowly, his countenance becoming more tense and concerned than she had ever seen it, "it is very serious, this that I must tell you."

Shelly felt dread rising inside her, but she said nothing.

"Perhaps I should not burden you with this, but I felt I must tell you because except for the Lord, no one else in life means so much to me."

The brown of his eyes had deepened almost to black with the special depth of feeling he was expressing.

Shelly started to speak, but he put his gloved fingertip to her lips to stop her.

"No, Shelly. Don't say anything now. Before I say what I must, I just wanted to remind you of your significance in my life."

Then taking both of her hands, he said, "The second thing I needed to tell you is . . . I am a member of the Communist party."

Chapter Ten

Demetri, a Party member? Shelly's mind could not accept the fact. But over and over his words banged in her head.

He can't be! It's impossible! Her mind kept remembering the things she'd heard about the Communist party, the terror she'd experienced since arriving here, the sight of broken, wasted Pavel. Demetri, a part of all that?

No! It couldn't be true.

"Please, Demetri, tell me it isn't so," she pleaded. "You were only joking, weren't you?"

"No, Shelly, I was not," he said heavily.

"But how can you be? I thought you were a Christian, that you love God. Was that all a farce?"

"No! No, Shelly, never that!" He released her mittened hands and gripped her shoulders.

An elderly man approached them, his head crouched low in the frayed collar of his ankle-length overcoat, and took the seat just in front of them. Demetri's eyes flashed a warning to Shelly about the dangers of their conversation being overheard, and he released his hold on her shoulders.

Both of them settled back into the seat, and sat together in strained silence until the bus left them at the train station. Darkness had fallen as they made their way to the train, and the street lights bathed the almost-deserted sidewalks with an iridescent bluish glare.

The railroad car they entered was empty and Shelly sat down with relief, glad for the privacy.

She gazed out the frosted window into the blackness beyond the station's glare.

The train lurched to a start, then sped along the tracks through the icy darkness.

Turning to Demetri, she said quietly, "I'd like an explanation if you're ready to tell me."

He nodded.

"It entails many things, so many things. I hope you will understand."

"I'll try to understand, Demetri," Shelly answered, her face full of doubt and confusion. "Truly, I'll try."

"Yes, I know you will, Shelly," he said, taking her hand. "You have a kind, generous heart.

"My grandfather was a Party member. He had high ideals, and sincerely wanted to better the country. He was a firm, stern old gentleman.

"Of course, my father followed in his footsteps. So as a youngster, the ideals of communism were a part of my daily life."

Shelly nodded her head, understanding so far.

"From the time I was nine until I became fifteen, I was a member of the Pioneers."

"That's similar to our American Boy Scouts, isn't it?" Shelly contributed.

"Yes, somewhat," Demetri agreed, "although it stresses socialism; I doubt that is so in America.

"Then I transferred to Komsomol, our Communist youth organization," he said.

"In my country," he continued, "we are usually slotted into scholastic groups by the time we're about fifteen. Because I showed special aptitude in writing, I later won entry into the university.

"I decided to make journalism my lifework, not only because of my ability but because I learned that a top journalist, like Party officials and managers of large factories, could earn about triple the average wage.

"I was selfish, trying to get all I could for myself. To do that I needed the Party and its advantages."

"What kind of advantages?"

"Oh, a good job and comfortable life; permits for the better apartments, access to restricted areas, stores with foods and other items not available to the general public, ability to buy a car without waiting for years, that sort of thing."

Shelly nodded. "What about your time at the university? Did you continue writing there as you'd hoped to?"

"Yes, and my decision to become a journalist, a really good one, became more firm than ever."

"What impressed you?"

"The fact that, in addition to the other things I've mentioned, a top reporter can boost his income with free-lance writing."

"But the main enticement was the great possibility of travel abroad."

"Couldn't you have done that anyway?"

"Usually it is difficult to get permission, and I wanted to make my future plans secure."

"What were your plans?" Shelly asked.

"Mainly, I wanted to be in a position to, as you say, 'live high on the hog.' A choice apartment and furnishings, the best food, travel to countries where I could purchase luxury items." Demetri looked disgusted with himself as he recited the list.

"I guess most of us have that attitude at some time in our lives," Shelly said, "and the majority of people never change."

"It is a miracle that I ever did," Demetri said. "I had begun to question inside myself some of the things I had been taught regarding communism, but I was ambitious and complied with the political conformity that is required by the Party."

He shook his head, "Even my writing was becoming false; my self-censorship made my work officially acceptable because I was determined that nothing, even my own probing mind, stand in the way of success."

Demetri continued, "At the university, our private conversations often revealed that many of us were beginning to puzzle over some of the issues, but even then we had to speak carefully, weighing our words."

"Why was that?" Shelly asked.

"Because, as a rule, we were never sure who the informer was in our group."

"But, Demetri," Shelly broke in, "you said it was a miracle that your attitude changed. What changed it?"

"We're obligated for two years of military service, so while I was in the university I was in the Reserve Officer Training and became a junior lieutenant at graduation.

"I did some free-lance work for the armed forces' newspaper after that; and last year while on assignment, I met one of my old friends from one of my university-days discussion groups.

"He is married now and invited me to his apartment for supper and a study group he thought would interest me."

"And did it?" Shelly asked when he paused.

"Very much," Demetri smiled. "It was a clandestine Bible study. Valali had become a Christian through the witness of his wife, Serafina, before their marriage.

"They were firm and happy in their trust in God. I had never known anyone before who had this great confidence, and I learned from them that Jesus loved me, that He had died for my sins."

There was a glow on Demetri's face as he said, "I met with them every night for the week I was in their area. By the time I returned to Moscow, I, too, was a follower of the Lord."

Shelly smiled back, happy to hear what he was relating, yet with deep questions still in her heart.

"Demetri," she asked haltingly, "I thought, I mean, how can you be a Christian and in the Party? I read that communist members are not permitted to attend church services."

"True. It would be dangerous to be seen there unless you are present as a KGB spy."

"What! You're a spy for them? That's why you attend the services?" Shelly lashed out at him, her words scathing.

"Shelly, no! You misunderstand. I said it would be dangerous unless one was. That's why I'm so cautious, why I hid with you the other evening in the barn.

"But it is the usual thing for spies to be in attendance. New converts coming into a group are often not what they seem."

A chill ran up Shelly's spine as she remembered the time of terror in the old barn.

"Demetri, how can you stay in the Communist party, knowing what it stands for, that it's anti-God?"

"I can't, Shelly; that is my problem, and it is not a simple one," he said sincerely, deep earnestness on his face.

"I have been seeking God's guidance as to how to proceed, but as yet the way has not been made clear."

"But why don't you just resign from the Party? Don't you feel sort of like . . . like a hypocrite?"

"I can understand your feeling so, Shelly, but secrecy and concealment are necessary for a while until I am absolutely sure of God's leading in this matter.

"And you must realize, secrecy and concealment are not necessarily the same as falsehood and duplicity."

"You're right, Demetri. I'm sorry for what I said."

"You need not be; it is right that you would think so."

"When I resign, they may confiscate my work papers, and

without them, regular employment is impossible.

"When Pavel was arrested, Pytor and Galina had their jobs and work papers taken from them because they had been assisting him with the printing. Also, they were forced to give up their apartment, so they moved back to my parents' home in Orensk. They get a bit of part-time employment, but it is not enough, so I began sending extra rubles to take care of them."

Demetri heaved a sigh. "If I have no sure income, what will happen to them and my mother? They would be destitute."

"What are you going to do?" Shelly asked, concerned for his dilemma.

"I do not know."

Shelly sat quietly, knowing she had no solutions to offer. This situation might be more serious than she realized. Would they possibly treat him as they did Pavel? What drastic consequences might he face when he left the Party?

"Shelly," Demetri said, breaking the silence and holding her hand close in his, "when I was newly saved, I intended to immediately resign from the Party, spending my time telling others the great news of Christ.

"It was a time of deep conflict in my soul because I was afraid I might be hesitating from the knowledge that I would lose my position and everything I had been working for. Perhaps even that I was in some way denying my Lord by my hesitation.

"One evening, after about a week of praying sincerely about the matter, I opened the Bible my friends had loaned me to continue my new habit of reading the Scriptures daily.

"But that night, something seemed wrong with my eyes. The pages were blurred. It concerned me greatly.

"Yet, as I turned the pages, wondering what had happened to me, one verse became clear, Jeremiah 29:11."

"What did it say?" Shelly asked, intrigued.

"It said, God had a plan for my life, for good, not evil.

"I felt it was God cautioning me to use great care and not do anything sudden or rash," Demetri explained.

"Were you able to read all right after that?"

"That night only one other portion was clear enough to read. I flipped through pages to make sure."

"And what was that?" Shelly asked, excitement stirring in her heart.

"It was in Psalm 50. 'Call upon me in the day of trouble; I

will deliver you and you shall glorify me.' "

Thank you, God, Shelly said silently, *for letting me know this.*

Aloud she said, "I'll not doubt you again, Demetri, and I'll be asking the Lord to guide you specifically in your decisions concerning this." There were tears in her lovely brown eyes when he met her gaze.

Demetri put his arm around her shoulder and pulled her to him until her head was resting on his shoulder. "Thank you for your prayers, Shelly, I shall deeply need them. We will trust our God together."

They sat silently for a while, content in the peace of each other's closeness as the train sped on to Orensk.

Later, when he left her at the Rozkalne door following the cold, moonlit walk from the station, she said, "Demetri, I hope it was all right; while you were talking to Pavel and the guards weren't noticing, I slipped a tiny booklet of Scripture verses into his pocket."

Because of the darkness, Shelly could not see Demetri's face, but she sensed his approval.

"Bless you, Shelly. What a joy and strength that book will be to him."

Demetri put his arms around her.

"No greater gift could he have received. If you do nothing more for the Lord but this one thing while you are here, it will be more than worth whatever the trip will have cost you."

The next night, during the evening meal with Aunt Tanya and Uncle Vladimer present, she told in detail about the sightseeing in Leningrad and the visit with Pavel.

But she kept secret Demetri's revelations of his continuing Party affiliation and his declaration of love for her.

Hearing about Pavel's poor appearance brought deep concern to Leonila about her husband, and to the Rozkalnes concerning Valentina.

Leonila voiced her worry to Shelly when they retired later to their room, and they prayed together for the safety of the imprisoned loved ones.

Chapter Eleven

The next morning Shelly was wakened in a still dark room by what sounded like hail hitting against the small window.

Pulling herself from the warm cocoon of covers, she crept over to look out.

Below, in the faint light from the setting moon, she saw the figure of someone in a long dark overcoat looking up in her direction.

Shelly watched as the figure's arm cocked, then thrust forward in a throwing motion that resulted in a clatter on the windowpane just inches from her face.

In a loud whisper she called, "Leonila! Leonila, come here quickly!"

Once beside her, Leonila looked down, then whispered excitedly, "I don't know how he got here, but it looks like Fyodor."

Turning, she rushed out the bedroom door and down the stairs into the darkness.

Feeling her way, Shelly followed her to the front door.

The flurry of commotion that ensued awoke Aunt Tanya and Uncle Vladimer. In moments they were beside Shelly.

When Aunt Tanya realized who had arrived, she hurried to the kitchen. Checking first to see that the inner shutters were tightly closed, she turned on a light and started water for tea.

The others led Fyodor to the kitchen and helped him to a chair. He looked frozen and was almost too exhausted to talk.

Uncle Vladimer helped him out of his coat while Aunt Tanya went for a blanket to wrap around him.

Startled at seeing Shelly, Fyodor evidently asked them who she was, and Uncle Vladimer immediately introduced her with a brief explanation. He acknowledged the greeting in English.

Tanya returned with a blanket, some tea and warmed soup left from supper. They all began to talk excitedly, and in deference to Shelly, all continued to use her language, even in this time of excitement.

Leonila said with tears on her cheeks, "Fyodor, I was afraid they would sentence you for years. Instead, they have released you. Thank God for answering our prayers."

"Yes, miraculously," he answered, holding the hot tea glass in both hands, savoring the warmth. "But I was not released exactly."

"What do you mean?" she asked. "You're here."

A slight smile formed on Fyodor's almost ashen lips; then he went on. "I feel as I'm sure the Apostle Paul did when the angel led him from the locked prison. My release was not supernatural in the same way, but to me it was as dramatic."

"My dear," Leonila asked, happiness and excitement on her face, "what happened?"

"I had been taken to the Commisar's office and lined up with a number of others. When I stood before him, I was told that I had been sentenced in absentia and was to be sent to the Polynarnyi Labor Camp in Murmansk Region for five years."

"Five years!" Leonila exclaimed.

Fyodor put the tea down and took her hand, holding it against the blanket that covered his chest. Then he continued, "When the Commisar summoned the guard to return me to my cell, a different one came than the one who had brought me. I didn't recognize him.

"Instead of returning me to my regular crowded cell, he shoved me into a small solitary one. I was feeling desperate, not having any way to get word to you, and worried that they might not tell you where they were sending me.

"Early the next morning, that same guard returned with another one and unlocked the door. 'Come out, Anatoli Meged,' one commanded. I crawled out and started to tell him I was not Anatoli Meged, but he yelled that talking by the prisoner is not permitted, and I should follow him.

"Because the other fellow had a small weapon pointed at me, I fell in between them and started down the corridor."

"Then what?" Leonila urged, when he paused.

"They escorted me to the main entrance where they gave me a set of outer clothing and overshoes. I was dumbfounded, sure there was a mistake," Fyodor said. "Then the one with the gun motioned me out the door while the other one said that I was wise to have signed a confession because now I was free.

"He said also that my release papers and a bit of food were in the coat pocket.

"I found myself outside in the paved courtyard in front of the prison entrance. The door was locked behind me, and the public sidewalk was before me. I walked away as fast as I could, discovering by the sign that I had been in Kreklon Prison in Garlonz."

Leonila threw her free arm around him, "Why, that's only ten miles from here. And all those weeks I did not know where you were!"

"No one paid attention to me," Fyodor continued then. "Only a few people were out on their way to work. I got to the edge of town as quickly as possible and checked the release papers; they were for an Anatoli Meged. The guard must have mistakenly put me in the cell where Meged had been before we were taken to the Commisar's office.

"I hid until dark when I started for Orensk. It was difficult going through the deep snow, but I was afraid to use the roadways or paths."

He paused, looking uncertain. "That was night before last, I believe.

"I arrived at our home just before dawn yesterday and found you gone, the house boarded up."

"Oh, Fyodor," Leonila said, caressing his cheek with her free hand.

"I forced a door open and spent the day on the bare floor. Everything was gone. They took it from you?" he asked Leonila.

When she nodded her head, he said, "This is the only place I felt sure you would be if you were still in Orensk."

Fyodor had given Uncle Vladimer a thankful look. "There was someone across the street who seemed to be watching your house until a few hours ago. I waited until sure they were gone."

"Fyodor, you must sleep now. We will talk more tomorrow."

With that he fell prostrated on the little cot in Aunt Natalia's room off the kitchen.

He was asleep almost immediately, Leonila sitting on the floor beside him wrapped in Natalia's shawl.

Shelly crept quietly back upstairs, making sure Ivan and Anna were well tucked in before she crawled back into her own bed. She was awed by what Fyodor had told them and lay staring into the faint darkness, shivering in her bed, remembering, wondering.

The next day, Fyodor was moved into the little upstairs room with his family, and Shelly brought her things to Aunt Natalia's room.

It was decided at the breakfast table that Fyodor would stay in bed that day, and he was too weak to protest.

"We have been spreading the word," Uncle Vladimer said, "that the birthday party is to be here tomorrow night. What a surprise our church will have when they discover our pastor is to speak to us."

"But what if the police should suspect and come to check?" Leonila asked, worry evident on her face. "If they recognize Fyodor, he will be taken back to prison. Surely the mistake has been discovered by now, and they will be watching his friends in Orensk."

"We have visited only the ones we are absolutely sure of," Uncle Vladimer said.

"Just in case, why not disguise him?" Shelly asked. "Make him look like an elderly lady. No one would suspect her of being him, at least just by seeing him."

The members arrived singly and in small groups over the period of two hours that evening. At the appointed time an old woman, stooped and leaning on a cane, entered from the direction of Aunt Natalia's room.

Her babushka was tied firmly under her chin, her black shawl wrapped closely around her thin shoulders. With a hacking cough, she took the chair Uncle Vladimer placed for her in a corner, her uneven skirt hem dangling over heavy grey stockings and worn shoes.

Later, as the frail-appearing figure raised her head, sat more erect and gave words of greeting, a sudden buzz of rejoicing voices filled the room as the people recognized their young pastor's voice.

Aunt Tanya had slipped into a space next to Shelly just inside the kitchen door. She now began singing loudly, in order to cover the revealing questions and praises from any unwanted ears of someone that might be lingering outside the house.

The others began to join in with words Shelly didn't understand but a tune familiar around the world: "Happy Birthday to you; happy birthday to you. Happy Birthday, dear Vladimer; Happy Birthday to you."

Earlier at supper, Uncle Vladimer had suggested that Fyodor share with the people some of the things that had happened to him since his arrest, so after several hymns of praise to God had been sung and he had read a number of Scripture passages, he began, with Aunt Tanya interpreting for Shelly.

"My dear friends, dear ones in Christ, how good it is to be with you again, joined in God's love.

"Knowing you were praying for me gave me great courage while I was in prison. I was sustained by that and the awareness that truly my life was in God's hands, that things could happen to me only by His permission.

"At first, I wondered why God would allow this to happen, but after thinking about it, I remembered the Scripture teachings in Acts 14:22 that we are to go through tribulations as God's children.

"In First Peter, we are told to rejoice when we are in heaviness, that our faith may be tried, for it is more precious than gold.

"When I learned I would probably face a long prison or labor camp sentence if I did not submit to my captives and sign a confession to antistate activities, there was in my heart a deep calm. I knew it was the peace that passes understanding that Jesus said He would give us."

Pastor Tens, still in the figure of an elderly woman, stood, smiling gently, "I was aware that I would probably face torture and possibly death, but His serenity was within me.

"They accused me of slandering the Soviet state and its social system, but we know I was only serving God and serving you, my congregation, by preaching of His great love to us and His provision of salvation through Jesus Christ's death.

"I felt sure that there would be some way for me to serve God even in that place if necessary."

He smiled again, "And God provided the way. There was another Christian in my cell; Gennadi arrived the same day I did.

"At first, as we prayed together and discussed God's Word, the other prisoners berated us and made fun. One of them reminded us that when Yuri Gagarin, our first astronaut, was in orbit, he hadn't found God anywhere up there.

"I told them that the God I serve isn't seen with human eyes and in the way Gagarin was looking.

"As I explained that we must search with the eyes of our spirit and receive the Lord into our hearts where He wishes to dwell, I noticed many of the others listening intently.

"The guard warned me to stop talking such nonsense or I would be reported, but the next day as discussion continued, several men in the cell repented and asked God to save them.

"That night was the time of my first beating."

Shelly immediately thought of Pavel's appearance and his weakness, and wondered if he had been beaten.

Seeing the shock and sorrow on all their faces, Fyodor said, "God told us we should not fear those who can harm our bodies. We are to be, as much as possible, strong and courageous, for He that is in us is greater than the one in the world.

"They hadn't given us any work to do at that place except the weekly cleaning of the latrine and scrubbing of the pails that we used in the cells, so there was time for discussions and to answer the questions of the men who were becoming interested in hearing God's Word."

Fyodor paused, and appearing very weak, sat down.

"Did you have a Bible with you, Pastor?" someone asked.

"For a few days, yes. In my pocket when I was arrested was a small New Testament that had been given to me several years ago by an American I met in Moscow as a teenager. I usually carry it with me because it is convenient to use and also helps me improve my English which I might need someday.

"They didn't search me, although they had confiscated the Bible I used at the church.

"I knew the Testament would be taken if it was discovered, so I took it out only when I felt sure no guards were around.

"I spent much time memorizing, too, glad it has been a habit. I knew I needed to get much more of the Scripture firmly in my mind for the time when I might not have it in printed form anymore."

Uncle Vladimer asked, "Did they take it from you?"

"Yes, after about a week. I do not know whether a guard noticed or an informer in my cell told them, but two guards came in and demanded it.

"When I didn't produce it, they searched the cell while we were in the courtyard. Twelve of us there were in that small cell, and only occasionally were we permitted out.

"They found the Testament inside a corner of my mattress. They took some pieces of bread some of the men had hidden also. But they left a small pouch of tobacco. Gennadi, who had been in other prisons, said it probably belonged to a favored one, an informer."

Shelly listened, imagining the incidents taking place where she and Demetri had visited Pavel, and understanding how they could happen.

"The guards taunted me when we returned," Fyodor continued. "They tore it in half and threw it in a trash basket they were making one of the prisoners carry to contain their finds. I asked God to forgive them, to open their hearts, for surely they did not realize it truly was the Word of God.

"I begged them to let me keep it, but they just laughed.

"That night, the beating was more severe than the other. But I was not the only one treated so. Often I heard others. And our Lord also was treated so."

Fyodor began singing then, and the others joined in:

Where He leads me I will follow,
Where He leads me I will follow,
I'll go with Him, with Him all the way.

Shelly wondered if she could face a situation like that without breaking and denying God if that's what they asked.

"What if communism should take over America someday?" she questioned herself. "Would I trust the Lord to give me strength to stand for my faith in Him no matter what happened?"

She brought her mind back to the present, hearing Aunt Tanya interpreting again as Fyodor answered another question.

"Yes, it is difficult to understand how humans can be so cruel to others, but the depravity of men without God seems to have no limits. I realized I was dealing with not just men but Satan himself.

"I saw and experienced the effects of much hatred in prison, but also the immeasurable, overwhelming love of God.

"During the few months I was there, I saw several guards and many prisoners give their lives to the Lord."

Fyodor smiled, "In order than I no longer be able to spread propaganda, as they called it, I was put in another cell, but also on a work detail in the prison kitchen. Of course, while I worked I preached to anyone who would listen.

"I was found out and transferred to the laundry. In that way, God's Word was spread in several prison areas.

"One day while we were eating our meager lunch, a fellow sitting near me pulled a small pouch of tobacco from his pocket with what looked like a little book.

"As I got up to move closer, he tore out a page and used it to roll a cigarette.

"I saw that what he had *was* a book, my Testament."

Shelly gasped, as did several others.

"I asked where he had gotten it. He said from the large outdoor trash bin when he was on clean-up detail.

"I begged him for it, but he laughed and said he needed it worse than I did."

Shelly thought, *If only that man had realized how much he did need what was in that little book.*

"I offered him the only thing they hadn't yet taken, my watch. I'd always kept it high on my arm under the sleeve. And I agreed to do his turn at latrine cleaning for the rest of our time there."

Uncle Vladimer asked, "Had he used many of the Testament's pages?"

"I'm not sure because he had found only half of it. But I had the books of Mark through Romans and most of Matthew.

"I was so thankful to have it, so very thankful. From then on, I spent all the time I was in my solitary cell praying, thanking God and memorizing. Fortunately, a tiny light burned part of the night.

"A week went by without any beatings, so when a guard unexpectedly opened my tiny cell and ordered me out, I was sure a beating was ahead.

"Instead, he took me to the commandant's office, where I was received cordially, an attitude which made me suspicious, although it was a welcome change.

"He said to me, 'Well, Comrade Tens, you will be glad to know that you are being sent to Wing Three and a much finer cell.' "

Questions formed in her mind as Shelly listened, questions as to why Fyodor would get uneasy because of better treatment.

Fyodor continued, "Another alert bell rang in my mind at his calling me *comrade*. I thought they must want something from me besides signing a false confession. I felt I had to be very cautious. And I was right.

"They wanted me to report to them what the prisoners in the new cell talked about, and what their attitudes were. In short, I was expected to become an informer. Of course I didn't agree, but I think they thought I would change my mind because of the privileges I might receive.

"I found the cell was a large one with about two dozen men, all of them new to me. They were wary of me at first, but after several evenings of talking about God's great love, they became more friendly and I noticed some of them listening while they played the chess and checker games they had devised from bits of paper and twigs.

"Several of the men came to me at various times and said they wanted to become Christians. There were such changes in the lives of these men that all the others noticed and were very impressed.

"The men who didn't believe continued to contend with me about the Bible, but they couldn't explain the changes they observed in the lives of the men newly saved.

"For a while we had a sympathetic guard who also listened to the discussions and warned us whenever another guard approached, so we could change to an accepted subject.

"Not even the informer, whoever he was, turned us in.

"The last night, before I was taken to the wrong cell, one of the men had asked if he could read my piece of Testament for a while. I had just slipped it to him before they came for me. I never saw any of them again because the next morning I was released.

"So even though I left, my Testament stayed behind for the men to read and memorize. God is good," Fyodor concluded with a smile.

"Amen," Uncle Vladimer said, as did several others.

Shelly decided she would appreciate her Bible a lot more than she had, and would start memorizing some portions. Just then she jumped as she heard loud pounding on the doors, accompanied by loud, harsh shouts.

Frightened, Shelly looked questioningly at Aunt Tanya, who had already risen.

"They're telling us to open up immediately; it's the police."

Someone began singing happy birthday again and everyone immediately joined in, singing loudly and clapping. Leonila assisted Fyodor with his unfamiliar skirts as they disappeared up the narrow stairs.

Several people hurriedly sat on the bottom steps while Aunt Tanya rushed to the kitchen table, pretending to be preparing to serve tea and cake.

Shelly joined her as Uncle Vladimer opened the door with a jovial, welcoming smile, gesturing the uniformed men inside as though they were expected guests.

At that moment the back door burst open and Shelly was suddenly faced with a blast of cold air and two menacing men in uniform, their boots covered with snow.

All Shelly could understand of their demands were the words *Fyodor Tens*.

Chapter Twelve

The police left after scrutinizing the faces of everyone present, not seeming at all convinced the gathering was only a birthday celebration. However, they did not search the house; instead, voiced dire threats as they went out the front door.

The thankful group prayed quietly together and then held whispered discussions as to what should be done to keep Pastor Tens hidden.

As they were drinking tea before leaving, Uncle Vladimer spoke, standing in the middle of the living room.

"He says," Aunt Tanya told Shelly, "that he knows of a safe place and will take Fyodor's family there tomorrow."

Fyodor appeared on the stairs and the folks sitting there moved to let him pass.

He had changed from the disguise; lifting his hand, he began to speak to them.

Demetri had come to sit by Shelly and quickly began translating.

"Jesus tells us in the book of Matthew that when we are persecuted because we are Christ's followers, we should be happy about it, because a large reward waits for us in heaven. He said also that we are needed here, that we make the world bearable by being its seasoning.

"Again, remember that we are reminded to not be afraid of those who can only kill our bodies, for they cannot touch our souls.

"And now, beloved friends in Christ, take these thoughts from our God's Word with you in your heart."

Fyodor lifted both hands in benediction, "And now may the awareness of God's presence be your strength." With a smile, he turned and slowly climbed the stairs.

Demetri said quietly to Shelly, "Mr. Rozkalne asked me to stay a while." He smiled, "I'm glad to have some extra time with you."

When the last person had left, Uncle Vladimer came to sit heavily in a chair across the table from them.

"I did not ask you to stay for social reasons, my boy," he said. "I need your help. We cannot wait until tomorrow to get Fyodor to a safer spot."

"Where are you taking him?" Shelly asked.

"Come, I show you," he said, standing. "Help me move the table, Demetri."

"Move that rug the table was sitting on," he nodded to Demetri, and went to remove a lantern from a shelf above the old cabinet.

He stepped over to them and lighted the lantern just as Demetri finished rolling the small rug out of the way, revealing a trapdoor.

"Open, please."

Demetri stooped and slipped his fingers into several holes placed along the door's edge. As he pulled, it opened easily, but with a loud squeaking of hinges.

"I must oil those," Uncle Vladimer said, starting down the crude wood steps. "Be careful; there is no railing and the steps are very steep."

"I'll go ahead and help you down, Shelly," Demetri said, stepping into the opening.

Shelly took the hand he offered and gingerly followed him down the narrow stairs.

She found that they were in a rather small cellar of bare earth, the floor hard-packed and smooth.

The light from the lantern revealed baskets and rough-hewn crates of apples and vegetables, potatoes, beets, carrots. In another area were many large cabbages and bulging burlap bags.

One wall had rough wood planks stacked on short sections of logs to form units of shelves which held jars of pickled vegetables and other preserved items.

Setting the lantern carefully on the floor near the preserves shelves, Uncle Vladimer began moving some of the straw piled high in a corner against some old bed springs.

Demetri went to help him, setting aside some cabbages half-hidden along the edge of the strawpile.

When they had uncovered the bedsprings, Uncle Vladimer pulled them away from the wall, revealing a hole the size of a low doorway hidden by a piece of tattered burlap hanging on the back of the springs.

Shelly picked up the lantern and took it to Uncle Vladimer.

Holding it ahead of him, he stooped through the opening.

"Careful," he said, "there are three steps down."

They followed him into a room similar to the food storage room.

"Years ago, during the purges when so many were imprisoned or murdered, I assisted my father and grandfather in digging out this extra room. They felt that even if we never needed it, someday someone would."

"Did your family need to use it?" Shelly asked.

"Nyet. But thankful to God, I am, that it is here now."

"And this is where you'll bring Fyodor?" Demetri asked.

"Yes, and Leonila and the little ones." Uncle Vladimer put the lantern on a table at the side of the room and Shelly saw three bunks made of planks positioned against the walls.

She crossed the room to look closer at the recesses at various levels in the walls, holding dishes, and a few wooden toys and chess and checker games. One deep recess held several filled oil lamps.

A covered pail sat in a corner; two chairs and some stools lined the other walls.

"It seems much warmer in here than in the other part of the celler," Shelly said, "almost as warm as upstairs."

"It is because we are farther underground, with an earth covering," Uncle Vladimer said. "Plenty warm they will be here bundled up in sweaters. If it should get colder, they can put on coats."

"What about air, Mr. Rozkalne?" Demetri asked.

"Is all right. We made vents opening up under part of the house. See, over there in ceiling. And one near floor under table leads to outside into garden shed. Is good circulation."

Picking up the lantern, he preceded them out of the earth room. Shelly went upstairs while the men concealed the opening by replacing the bedsprings and straw.

In the kitchen, Aunt Tanya was assembling bread and cheese in a basket with the tinned fish Shelly had purchased for Valentina's homecoming.

"What can I do to help?" Shelly asked.

"I have hot water almost ready. You may bring that pail over there and get some rags from the bottom drawer in Mama's room.

We will clean the furniture in the secret place to make ready to bring the bedding down tomorrow."

Remembering the beds made of planks, Shelly said, "Please take the mattress from my cot for the children, Aunt Tanya."

"Bless you, Shelly, but that won't be necessary. Come, I show you," she answered, leading the way to the room where she and Uncle Vladimer slept.

Pulling back a corner of the mattress, she said, "An extra one, thin but comfortable, has been kept here many years in case of emergency. The same on the beds upstairs."

Opening the top of an old trunk, she revealed a pile of comforters and pillows. "We have been prepared, but until now have used these only on the parlor floor for overnight guests."

Aunt Tanya continued gravely, "If we are to care for our families and be able to share with others during bad times, whatever they are, we must prepare extra necessities for daily life."

It was almost 3 a.m. when they returned from the cellar, content that the room was as tidy as it could be.

"Shelly, you must sleep now for a few hours. Vladimer will leave for work soon after that, and I have promised to work to fill the place of a lady who is ill. We must make everything appear as normal here as possible."

She hugged Shelly before giving her a gentle push toward Aunt Natalia's door. "We will be depending on you and Demetri to help Fyodor's family get situated. The men have been out checking the vent holes and doing some other necessary things. They have brought the Tens' trunk here to the kitchen and will move it downstairs."

Shelly was awakened by the sound of voices talking quietly in the kitchen. She dressed hurriedly, and remembering the work ahead, tied the thick waves of her brown hair back with a ribbon.

She found Leonila and Aunt Tanya at the table. Uncle Vladimer, going out the back door, waved cheerfully.

As Shelly sat down, Demetri came in from the parlor, trying to stifle a yawn.

"You're up bright and early," he teased Shelly. "You don't even look tired."

"I think I'm excited about the room we're to get ready today," she said. "The idea is full of intrigue."

"Breakfast is ready for everyone," Aunt Tanya said. "I will be home as early as possible this afternoon. Anything you need me to shop for Leonila? Shelly?"

They both shook their heads and Leonila said, "I cannot tell you how thankful I am that you're sharing your home with us." Tears filled her blue eyes.

Aunt Tanya, bundled in her coat, hugged Leonila. "I thank God we were prepared, dear."

Leonila fixed a tray for her husband and the children, and Demetri carried it upstairs for her while Shelly took breakfast to Aunt Natalia.

Then hurrying upstairs after straightening the kitchen, they removed the covers from the beds.

Demetri removed the extra mattress from the bed that had been Shelly's and carried it to the kitchen, ready to go to the secret room.

"Look, Shelly," Leonila said when they rolled back the mattress on the larger bed, "there are two narrow ones here."

"They'll be just right, I think, for the two narrower beds I saw down there. I suppose they were made especially for them."

The men carried the mattresses down while the young women hurriedly remade the beds.

"Aunt Tanya showed me extra bedding in a chest in her room," Shelly said, "and pillows with extra comforters in Aunt Natalia's. We could hand the things down when they have the mattresses in place. I don't like the thought of carrying them down those steep, narrow stairs."

"While you get those out," Leonila said, "I'll get our clothes ready. They are still mostly packed in the box and trunk so they'll be quick to move."

The secret room began to take on a homey, comfortable atmosphere when the plank beds were made up, a basket of food sat ready on one end of the table, and large canning jars of water were placed in one of the wall recesses above the table.

Leonila had hung her family's coats and hats on pegs protruding from the earthen wall and lined their boots up on the floor beneath them. Several of Fyodor's books that she had been able to hide among the children's things when being forced to leave her home were at the other end of the table in the glow of an oil lamp.

Ivan and Anna had scampered down the stairs after them and were dancing around the room, laughing as if it was great fun.

"One good thing about being down here," Leonila said, "they probably won't have to be quiet as before."

Fyodor put his arm around her, "I think we must be cautious

still. The sounds may penetrate more than we think, possibly through the vent areas."

Shelly had gone up into the kitchen then to get Leonila's Bible and some blank paper, so she and Fyodor could continue with the copying.

She had just put her foot on the top step to start back down when the knock came at the kitchen door.

Gripped with fear, her heart seemed to stop for a moment as she remembered the previous night.

She tried to think quickly. Her first impulse was to go down the stairs, pulling the door closed after her so she wouldn't have to face whoever was knocking. But the trapdoor would be obvious with the table and rug pulled aside.

Hurrying as fast as she could down the steep stairs, she called in a loud whisper, "Demetri! Hurry!"

Then reaching the room opening, she gasped, "Demetri! Someone's at the door!"

Leonila shushed the children when she saw the look on Shelly's face.

"What is it?" Demetri asked, taking the Bible and paper from her and handing them to Leonila.

"The door. Someone's at the door."

With a quick nod of understanding, he grabbed her hand, pulling her behind him into the cellar. Placing the bedspring over the little entrance, he hurriedly threw straw against it.

They rushed up the steep steps and Demetri closed the trapdoor. Shelly pulled the rug over it, and they lifted the table to its usual place.

The knocking continued, but Shelly realized now that it was insistent, but not as loud and demanding as that of the night before.

Grabbing a cloth, she placed it over her Testament and stack of paper and picked up a pan of potatoes and a knife as Demetri went to the door.

A stooped, elderly man in a tattered coat, the collar pinned up against the cold, shuffled inside when Demetri threw the door open.

"Mr. Belan!" Demetri said.

Shelly recognized him as the old gentleman who had told Aunt Tanya of the church meeting the day they were shopping. She had noticed him, too, last night sitting in a corner during the birthday party.

While Demetri was helping him remove his coat, he said, "He

tells me he's here on an errand for the Lord. He knew the family might be away but he hoped you might be here. He has something to show us."

Shelly smiled at the old gentleman and sat at the table where he was carefully unfolding a small bundle of cloth he had removed from inside his sweater.

Although it was burned to a tattered blackness, the object had obviously been a book. The pages broke apart into crisp, sooty pieces as, with great care, Mr. Belan's gnarled fingers opened it slowly near the middle where some of the pages had portions still intact.

Shelly saw that it had been a Bible and wondered what had happened to cause it to be burned.

Mr. Belan and Demetri talked softly for a few minutes; then Victor rose to go.

"Ask him if he wouldn't stay for lunch with us, or at least have some tea," Shelly said.

After Demetri asked him, the old gentleman smiled at Shelly and shook his head.

"He said that after what happened last night, someone may be watching, but he felt this was too important to wait and thought no one would think anything of an old man coming for a visit."

After Mr. Belan had limped out the door, Shelly said, "Will you please go down and let Leonila and Fyodor know everything's all right? They're probably worried about us."

When he returned, she had put bread and cheese on the table and he sat across from her.

"What happened to Mr. Belan's Bible?" Shelly asked.

"It wasn't his; he found it. Remember Fyodor telling us about his Bible being taken in prison and thrown in the trash?"

"Yes," Shelly said, cutting slices of bread and cheese and putting it on a small plate for him.

"Well, Mr. Belan often goes out to the dump to search for usable items to sell. That is how he makes his living. When he heard Fyodor mention his Bible, he remembered seeing a truck there one day with two uniformed men setting fire to the things they had thrown out.

"He went out there this morning, wondering if possibly that could be the spot where they were destroying confiscated Bibles.

"The fragments he found among the ashes appeared to be those of books, but this was the only one he could find that was intact at all. He planned to go every day and watch, but he turned his ankle on something out there.

"That's why he came here. He knew the Rozkalnes were absolutely trustworthy."

Shelly said, "If we could be there when they start the fire, maybe we could put it out and save the Bibles."

"We?" Demetri asked.

"Sure, why don't we try? Unless you won't be here."

"I still have about a week fairly free, Shelly, but we would easily attract attention out there."

"Maybe not. If Mr. Belan is in the habit of going to the dump, perhaps other old people do also."

"We're hardly old folks, Shelly."

"We could be. Remember Fyodor last night," she said.

Demetri chuckled, "You are suggesting we disguise ourselves?"

"Yes, let's do it," Shelly said, her eyes sparkling. "We might really be able to accomplish something; beat the wrongdoers at their own game. It might be fun, too."

"Also, dangerous, Shelly. Do you understand that?"

"Yes, Demetri, I do," she said, sobering, remembering the night in the barn. "But we can be careful. Surely, no one would suspect an old couple picking through junk of being subversive. Let's ask Leonila and Fyodor what they think about it."

Early the next morning, a stooped man in a pulled-down hat and a too-large overcoat escorted a woman bundled in shawls over a coat that flapped around the heavy grey wool socks showing above her old overshoes. On her arm hung two empty string bags.

Her other arm was slipped through the crook of his elbow where he carried a rolled blanket. His free hand clasped the top of a cane with which he seemed to steady himself.

Shelly was relieved when they reached the far edge of town and started down a rough path through the snow.

"I'm glad everyone seemed in too much of a hurry to pay any attention to us," she said.

"I, too," Demetri said, straightening and walking erectly. Lifting the cane he let it swing in his hand. "We can walk faster as long as no one is around. It will take us about an hour, I think."

Large white snow mounds camouflaging piles of refuse spar-

kled in the rays of the rising sun when they reached their destination.

Around the edges of some mounds the wind had blown the
snow away, revealing odds and ends of discards, and several piles
of objects had not yet been covered by the snow.

"Victor said the truck he had seen came in at the far left edge
of the area where the road to Kreklon passes. We can check these
recent dumpings as we pass them on our way over there."

They were scanning an array of items near the middle of the
area when Shelly said, "Demetri, listen! Something's coming."

A grinding of gears preceded the appearance of a dark van over
a rise near the area Mr. Belan had mentioned.

"Bend over, quickly," Demetri said, suddenly taking on the
appearance of a feeble old man poking among the debris with his
cane.

Shelly pulled the shawl down over her face and picked up a
piece of metal, seeming very interested in it.

"Good, you're doing fine, Shelly. Keep it up," Demetri said,
shuffling forward so he could get a better view of the arrivals, yet
trying to appear absorbed in the scattered items on the ground.

Peering cautiously out from the edge of her shawl, Shelly saw
a young man in a tan overcoat and cap with red collar tabs and
hatband jump from the van and hurry around to the back where he
opened the door and dragged out several boxes which he let fall
on the ground. Tossing something from his hand toward the boxes
as he jumped back inside out of the cold, he slammed the door and
the van roared off.

After the vehicle disappeared beyond the rise of snowy ground,
Demetri shouted, "Come!" and began to run toward the spot.

Shelly tried to hold up the long coat hem as she struggled
through the snow after him.

She saw tiny flames beginning to lick over the edge of one of
the boxes in the still air as the sound of the motor died in the
distance.

By the time she reached him, Demetri had smothered the flames
with snow and his blanket. She saw that indeed the boxes contained
books, mostly Bibles and hymnals.

"Mr. Belan was right, Demetri!" she exclaimed.

"We must hurry, Shelly, before anyone comes," he said. Shaking out the blanket and spreading it on the ground, he thrust some
cloths toward her.

"Wrap as many Bibles as you can together in one of these and stuff them in your string bags."

They worked quickly, glancing around every few moments to make sure they were still alone.

Everything she couldn't get into her bags, Demetri piled in the blanket and gathered it up as firmly as possible.

Placing the bundle on a mound of snow away from the now-empty boxes, he set the boxes afire and threw several pieces of junk around them.

"Come," he said, hanging one of the heavy bags over his arm and picking up the blanket bundle.

Shelly took the other net bag and followed him around the perimeter of the dump to the path back to Orensk, passing several elderly people who were now wandering through the piles of refuse.

By the time they reached Uncle Vladimer's house, Shelly's bag, stretched to capacity, was dragging along on the snow; its weight had become too much for her to manage otherwise.

After they dropped their bundles of precious cargo on the kitchen floor and removed their boots, Demetri opened the trapdoor and went down to get Fyodor.

The two young men carried the bundles of books down into the hidden room.

Shelly had hung the coat and shawls on a peg and was smoothing her hair when Demetri reappeared. He slipped into his boots; then, putting his hands on her shoulders, he said, "I must go now, Shelly. Galina told me yesterday that she needed to talk with me privately, and she has no work today. She seemed very worried."

Gently he pulled her against him. "My mother asked me to bring you to supper again soon. May I come for you this evening?"

"Yes," Shelly said against his chest, "I would like that."

Tipping her chin upward with his finger, he kissed her softly. "I love you, Shelly. Remember it always, whatever happens."

During the next few hours, while she sat at the kitchen table copying sheet after sheet from her Testament, her mind kept wandering to thoughts of Demetri and her feelings for him.

When Leonila came cautiously upstairs to make tea and sandwiches for her family, she said, "Shelly, you do not understand, I am sure, what a wonderful thing you and Demetri did going to rescue the books. It will mean so much to our church."

Shelly smiled, "There are five Bibles in perfect condition and ten more only partly damaged. I'm glad I could help; I am realizing more and more what some Christians go through just getting a Bible to read."

"Not only can more in our church have them now," Leonila said, "but they can also start copying as we are. They can purchase paper for their own use instead of for us. We will find some way to get some."

"Which reminds me," Shelly said, "I have only a few sheets left."

"The word has been passed through the church that each one purchase a small amount from time to time, as much as they can afford. That way no suspicion will be aroused."

After Leonila had returned to the cellar, Shelly finished copying on the sheets she had, then peeled potatoes and chopped the cabbage she knew Aunt Tanya intended to use for supper.

When Demetri arrived that evening, she greeted him in soft blue sweater and slacks, her hair falling over her shoulders in soft waves.

He grinned appreciatively at her, and as he helped her on with her coat, whispered, "You're absolutely lovely, Shelly."

The snow glinted with light from the slice of moon relieving the darkness. They walked arm in arm, content in each other's company.

"Demetri, were you able to help Galina? Did she tell you what was troubling her?"

"Yes, she did, Shelly," he answered, "but I don't know if I can help the situation."

"May I know what's wrong?"

"She said Pytor has been going out every night right after supper the past week, and when he returns he is pale and shaking.

"He won't tell her what is bothering him or where he goes. The other night, she followed him; he went to the local KGB headquarters."

"You think he's an informer?"

"I don't know what to think, Shelly. But I've decided to confront him if it happens again."

Chapter Thirteen

Shelly enjoyed being in the small home where Demetri had spent his childhood. The company was warm and welcoming around the supper table with his mother and Galina and Pytor.

When the conversation led to Fyodor's family, Mrs. Barinov said, "Very concerned I am. Pastor will be returned to jail if he's found, and the children may be taken." She shook her head sadly.

"Take the children?" Shelly asked.

"Many families are being split up," Galina said. "The Party has been taking stern measures in recent years against religion."

Demetri nodded. "I covered a meeting of the officials of Komsomol for their paper some time ago, where the Komsomol's chief told them they were not trying hard enough to stamp out religion."

Smiling gently at his mother, he continued, "And she is correct about the children. Pastukhov said they should put more effort into instilling atheism into every child, and should concentrate on children of believers."

"I, too, have recently heard they often take the children of uncooperative believers and put them in state homes," Pytor said. "Indoctrination there is very rigid."

Mrs. Barinov shook her head sadly, "First the Bibles; now the children."

"Concerning Bibles," Demetri said, "Shelly and I rescued some confiscated ones, Galina. I wondered if you and Pytor and mother would do some copying as Shelly and Leonila have been?"

"Of course," Pytor and Galina answered.

"If only I had a typewriter, it would really speed up the work," Shelly said.

Demetri nodded, "But typewriters are difficult to obtain, and must be registered with the authorities."

Pytor laughed dryly. "Can you not just imagine their faces if we asked to get one for copying the Scriptures?"

"I just remembered something," Galina broke in. "Paval had an old one with an English keyboard in his printshop storeroom. He salvaged it from discards near the foreign apartment complex when he was in Moscow years ago. He was planning to repair it and perhaps sell it."

"The authorities may have sealed the shop when he was arrested," Demetri said.

"They locked it and took the keys," Galina said, "but I don't think they took anything; at least while I was there, they did not."

"We had hoped," Pytor said, "that we or Pavel would be allowed to open it again. It would give both of us work, and we would not be a burden on your salary, Demetri."

"Well, we have keys to a back door if we wanted to get in," Galina said. "I had extras made because I was fearful of the authorities closing the shop."

"You haven't been in there, have you?" Pytor asked.

"No, there was no reason. We could hardly have tried to do any work because everyone knew Pavel had been arrested and the shop closed."

"I don't want you going in now, either," Pytor said gruffly. "We don't need more problems."

"But, Pytor . . ." she began.

"No!" he half-shouted, leaving the table. "No!"

It was very quiet in the kitchen for several minutes.

"I'm sorry, Shelly," Galina said. "I don't know what has come over him. Please forgive us for making you uncomfortable."

"Don't be concerned about that, Galina. I understand."

Turning to Demetri, Shelly said, "I've spent so little time with Aunt Tanya and Uncle Vladimer, I'd like to go home early this evening."

To Galina and Mrs. Barinov she smiled, "I've enjoyed my time with you. Thank you for inviting me again."

Demetri nodded and went for her coat. She hugged Mrs. Barinov warmly as she said her goodbyes.

She and Demetri had just reached the walk in front of the house when, hearing the door open, they turned to see Pytor coming out.

"Pytor," Demetri called, "I want to talk to you for a moment."

"Nyet!" Pytor brushed past them and started down the road, walking fast.

"Excuse me, Shelly," Demetri said, rushing after him. "Pytor!"

Pytor increased his pace along the snowy walk, but Demetri soon had him by the arm, halting him.

Shelly could hear Demetri's voice harsh and questioning, and Pytor's rough, firm answers.

Demetri's voice kept pressing, and Pytor's tones were quieting, halting, low. Then suddenly Demetri's arms were around his brother-in-law.

They stood there for what seemed a long time to Shelly before Pytor walked on, his shoulders hunched. Demetri came back to where she stood waiting.

"What's wrong, Demetri?"

"Oh, Shelly, I hesitate to even suggest to you what is wrong. And I'm not at all sure what to do."

Shelly thought she heard a sob in his voice and put her arm through his, looking up at him.

"Please, Demetri, share this with me."

"All right, Shelly, perhaps I should," Demetri's voice faded into a groan. "You can then be praying about it; how much we need to pray."

They began walking in the opposite direction Pytor had taken.

"My heart aches for him," Demetri said. "I don't know how he bears it. I wonder if I would be that strong."

"What is it, Demetri?"

"It began several weeks ago. He received a summons to be at the local KGB headquarters that night. Galina was shopping and Mother was napping, so they were unaware.

"When he got there, they began questioning him about why he had not left the church. They thought he had been warned enough by Pavel's imprisonment and the loss of his own job, and would have taken the hint by now.

"They kept harassing and taunting him for several hours. When they finally let him go, they demanded that he return the next evening at the same time."

"And he went?"

"Yes, of course. And the next night was the same, except they said that if he hadn't decided to leave the church by report time the next night, they would find a way to convince him. That night they beat him."

"Demetri, how could they?"

"Evidently they did not find it difficult," he answered between clinched teeth. "They have kept it up every night since, for hours at a time."

"Why does he continue to go back?" Shelly cried.

"He has little choice. They threatened that if he does not, they will send him to a distant labor camp. They suggested worse for Galina."

Shelly felt as though something were tightening around her chest, making it difficult to breathe.

"Why didn't he tell Galina?"

"They said if he tells anyone, even his wife, what is happening, it would mean his life. And they have learned to beat in such ways that there is little obvious evidence. He is afraid he may not be able to hold out; he has been suffering in silence."

Demetri was quiet for a few moments as they walked along, their boots crunching on the snow. Shelly, too, was absorbed in thought, fearing for these new friends.

Then Demetri spoke. "Once when I was at the university, a letter from one of my friends here mentioned that he happened to pass the KGB headquarters late one night and thought he heard screams coming from the basement below the building. I thought he was imagining things and didn't give it a second thought. Now . . ."

"Can't he go away somewhere?"

Demetri didn't seem to hear her. "Now they're trying to force him to give them the names of everyone in the church and tell them everything that goes on in the meetings.

"He refused to give any names, and when he partly cooperated by giving the Scriptures and message line, telling them of God's love, they just beat him more savagely."

"Can't we help him get away?" Shelly asked, her cheeks hurting from the tears freezing on them.

"If he went into hiding, they would probably take Galina, even Mother. He knows that, so he stays. He's going to collapse soon, I fear."

Aunt Tanya and Uncle Vladimer had finished supper and were sitting at the cleared table, copying from two of the Bibles brought in from the dump that morning.

"We both were able to purchase paper today," Aunt Tanya said, "and what a blessed surpise when Fyodor showed us the treasure you found this morning."

Demetri left and Shelly joined them at the table. "I want you to purchase some more paper for me tomorrow, Uncle Vladimer, if there is another place where you can get some. I'll give you the money tonight so I can have a real part in this."

"Nyet, Shelly, it would be too soon; they would get suspicious and probably report it. You will use some of this for now, and soon I will try to go into Cragow and buy some there."

"You and Demetri both seemed very subdued when you came in," Aunt Tanya remarked. "Is something wrong?"

Remembering brought horror to Shelly's heart. "He told me about . . . about someone he knows, a Christian, who is being beaten because he won't inform on his friends."

"Did he say who it is?" Aunt Tanya asked, concern on her face.

"The man was warned to not tell anyone, but he did share it with Demetri. I don't think I should say."

"That's right, little one," Uncle Vladimer said quietly, "better it is to be silent when you can. Bad times these are, when neighbor is urged to spy against neighbor."

Reaching out to put a hand on his wife's, he said, "So many Christian families are troubled right now. We are fortunate we can look forward to our Valentina's release soon."

"Today, yes, a card came from her," Aunt Tanya said brightening. "They told her she may plan to come home after the new year begins."

"And we received a gift today, also in the mail," Uncle Vladimer said. "Bring it, Tanya."

To Shelly he said, "Is from my sister in far-off Yakutak."

"It was a strange note she sent with it," said Aunt Tanya, handing him a square, neatly wrapped, cloth-covered package. "Not at all like her."

Opening a small decorated sheet of paper, Uncle Vladimer read, translating, "Early greetings for the coming new year and in honor of the great Party of our Mother Russia."

"Of course," Aunt Tanya said, "she may have been trying to fool any censors."

Uncle Vladimer said, "Is a special cake made with dried fruits, like our mother made." He smiled, reminiscing.

"We will enjoy some tonight," Uncle Vladimer said, "and save half for when our Valentina is home again. Shelly will take some down to Fyoder's family. A knife, please, Tanya."

She brought a large knife and some plates, then started to prepare tea.

Carefully Uncle Vladimer unfolded the cloth from a dark, moist cake.

Sliding the knife down through the cake's center, he suddenly stopped, a quizzical look on his face. Then, removing the knife upward, he reinserted it and pulled the two halves of cake apart.

A small glass vial protruded from one half.

Removing it and cleaning it of cake particles, he unscrewed the top and pulled out a tiny roll of paper.

Carefully, he unrolled it and read, again translating for Shelly.

Our son, Stefan, a fine Christian lad, died under mysterious circumstances while in the military. They said accidental electrocution. When coffin sent home, sealed, we opened. Unmistakably, he was tortured to his death. Satan is stalking our land. We must pray, pray. Does anyone outside know? Do they pray for us?

Uncle Vladimer finished with a groaning sob, tears running down his face. Aunt Tanya reached across to his hand to comfort him.

Shelly, tears filling her eyes, went to him and put her arms around him.

"I'm sorry, Uncle Vladimer; I'm so sorry," she said, leaning against his shoulder.

Shelly wondered how much these people could stand without breaking. She marveled that they were not lashing out at God or questioning why He didn't do something to stop this terror.

Almost as though he had read her mind, Uncle Vladimer said, "God's Word tells us in First Peter 4:12 that we should not be surprised at the painful trials we will suffer. Christ suffered, and as His followers, we must expect it."

Turning to look at her, he added, "And don't think harshly of those doing the persecuting. Pray for them that they will eventually realize God's love for them."

Getting heavily to his feet, he said, "Come, let us all go down and join Fyodor's family for a time of prayer together. Then," he smiled gently, "we will have cake and tea together, and sing a song with the little ones."

Later, going up to the room under the eaves where she was sleeping again since Fyodor's family had moved, Shelly's mind was heavy with the troubles suffered by the people she had met since coming here.

But while she knelt beside her bed praying, she rememb~~
again the verse, *Greater is he that is in you than he that is in*
world.

"Lord, show me some practical way to help these dear ones."
And as she slipped under the covers, she added half-aloud, "Even
if it doesn't seem practical to anyone else."

Shelly wasn't sure how long she had been asleep when the
knocking began. She jerked up to a sitting position. *Oh, no,* she
thought, *not again.*

The knocking quickly changed to pounding, accompanied by
harsh voices shouting demands.

Her first thought was of Fyodor's family and the Bibles.

Thankful she had brought her Testament upstairs with her, she
hurriedly pulled on her robe and slipped the little book into a
pocket, stuffing a silk scarf in over it.

She heard the front door thrown open, slamming back against
the wall with a crash. A cry from Aunt Tanya reached her ears.

Wondering frantically what to do, Shelly tied her robe sash and
slipped into her slippers.

By that time, heavily booted feet were stomping up the stairs,
approaching her room.

Chapter Fourteen

The uniformed man entering the room smiled with surprise when, in the glare of the light he had just switched on, he saw her crouching on the bed.

Striding over to her, he ran his hand over the loose waves tumbling over her shoulders, his smile changing to a leer.

Her heart thumping madly, Shelly jumped up, slid under his arm, dashed across the room and out the door.

His loud guffaw followed her as she stumbled down the stairs to the lamp-lit parlor.

Shelly ran to Aunt Tanya who stood in her nightgown in the circle of Uncle Vladimer's arm near the closed but sagging door.

He noticed her quick glance toward the kitchen where the table ꟷod in the middle of the room, firmly centered on the rug.

"Is all right," he said quietly, putting his free arm around her.

"What's happening?" she whispered quaveringly as two other ꟷrode in from the direction of Aunt Natalia's room.

"ꟷey're searching the house," Aunt Tanya said.

"ꟷ think we hide some fugitive," Uncle Vladimer said ꟷancing disdainfully at the men, repeating his statements

ꟷfould I hide in this humble place? Would I risk my neck ꟷlse?" He laughed sarcastically.

ꟷtheꟷre talking together now, seeming to disagree. As ꟷrooꟷr clumped down the stairway from the upstairs ꟷm spoke harshly to Uncle Vladimer.

ꟷsaid ꟷed across Vladimer's wide chest to Shelly, "He ꟷand ꟷmer has the fugitive Tens hidden somewhere

ꟷand ꟷwhere he is."

ꟷand ꟷdimer said quietly, shrugging his shoulders

114

Before Shelly realized what was happening, the two men stepped forward and pushed her and Aunt Tanya away from Uncle Vladimer. Then grabbing him by the arms, they turned him toward the door.

Aunt Tanya cried out but they ignored her.

"Keep on with your work, little one," Uncle Vladimer said quietly as they shoved her away from him.

Shelly watched in horror as they hustled him out the door into the dark, barefooted and clad only in the long underwear in which he had been sleeping.

They watched out the open door as he was marched through falling snow to a van where he was unceremoniously shoved through its back door. It was slammed after him and they drove away.

"Stukachi!" Aunt Tanya said contemptuously through her tears, trying to close the door.

Shelly helped her swing it into place on its loosened hinges.

"Stukachi?"

"Informers, squealers. Someone informed to the KGB on Vladimer."

After spending a long time in prayer and trying to comfort one another, Shelly once again climbed the stairs after Aunt Tanya insisted she go back to bed. Shelly wondered if perhaps Demetri's brother-in-law may have finally cracked under the mental strain and beatings.

Shelly was unable to sleep any more that night and spent the time tossing and turning and praying. Her thoughts were much on Demetri, also, and any possibility of a life together they might have. Everything seemed so hopeless.

At dawn she dressed and went downstairs to find Aunt Tanya already up and preparing a package of Uncle Vladimer's clothes.

"They said they were taking him to the local KGB headquarters for questioning. If he is not home in a few hours, I will take these to him." Worry was heavy on her face.

The words *KGB headquarters* hit Shelly's mind like a gong, reminding her of Pytor's mistreatment.

"Not Uncle Vladimer, Lord," she prayed silently. "Please not Uncle Vladimer, too."

Shelly put water on to heat for the breakfast of tea and mush, then brought the container of milk from outside the door to thaw some for the children.

As she readied a tray for Fyodor's family and a small one for

Aunt Natalia, she asked, "Would you like me to go with you to take Uncle Vladimer's things?"

Aunt Tanya tried to smile through the tears that filled her eyes. "Nyet. You stay. Continue the copying. That is more important than my need of fellowship."

Though neither of them felt hungry, they drank tea together, then prepared the evening's vegetables and tidied the house until it was time to take breakfast to the cellar.

Leonila and Fyodor had been awakened earlier by the commotion and now were dismayed to learn that Vladimer had been arrested because of them.

"If only we knew somewhere else to go," Leonila said, deeply troubled.

"It would not help now," Fyodor said, putting his arm around her, the other around Aunt Tanya. "Even if I turned myself in, and I cannot because of you and the children, they would still convict him."

He smiled toward Shelly and his two youngsters, "Let us pray together. Only God can help in this."

They knelt along one of the cots and Fyodor prayed aloud: "O God, our Father, our Lord and Savior, our only hope in time of need, help now our dear ones, Vladimer and his Valentina, in prison because they love you.

"Hear our prayers for them. Keep their minds strong and clear. Give them the ability to recall your Word that it may strengthen and comfort them. Give them assurance of your care and your presence. May they have opportunity to tell someone there in the prison of your love. And for Tanya and Shelly I ask your strength and wisdom. For my family, Heavenly Father, I ask your guidance as to what we are to do, where we are to go to most honor you. Amen."

When Aunt Tanya had left, Shelly took the sheaf of paper from the breadbox where they'd hidden it under the bread and sat at the table to continue copying her New Testament.

She wished again she had a typewriter and decided to ask Demetri if he thought there was some way to get the one from Pavel's storeroom without causing problems for anyone.

As the afternoon had worn on, Shelly had become concerned, wondering why Aunt Tanya was so long returning.

Shelly had taken jars of fresh water down to Fyodor's family, and because Uncle Vladimer wasn't there, insisted on taking out their refuse pail.

She was taking it from Fyodor, who had carried it to the top of the trapdoor stairs, when Aunt Tanya arrived. Galina was with her.

"I met her just outside, coming to see you, Shelly."

"Demetri was called away on an assignment this afternoon; the journalist who was supposed to go was in an accident," Galina said. "Our phone was out of order for a few hours, and he had to rush to catch the train. He said you were expecting him this evening."

"Oh," Shelly said disappointedly. "Will he be gone long?"

"He wasn't sure, but probably about two weeks. He is to accompany another young athletic team to Helsinki to do a story on their amateur games."

"Two weeks!" Shelly said. "Then I won't have much more time with him. My visa will be up not long after that."

Galina put her arm around her. "You two have become important to each other, haven't you?" she asked quietly while Aunt Tanya went into her mother's room.

Shelly nodded, "Very important." She put on her boots and coat and went outside with the refuse pail.

When she came back in, Galina was fixing tea. Aunt Tanya was sitting dejectedly at the table.

Shelly asked, "Will Uncle Vladimer be here later?"

Aunt Tanya shook her head, covering her face with her hand. "They wouldn't let me see him," she answered, her voice catching on a sob. "They weren't even going to take his clothes at first."

She sighed deeply, raising her head. "They said Vladimir is being held for trial, but they would not tell me when it is to be held, or where."

"Oh, Aunt Tanya, and I was upset at not getting to see Demetri for a while. Isn't there some legal way to force them to tell you?"

Aunt Tanya's short, harsh laugh was a sound of disgust. "Here, even when a person is sentenced after a trial, the legal appeal is allowed only to the prosecutor to press for a harder sentence, not to the prisoner for justice."

The situation in this place Shelly had so longed to visit was beginning to feel like a tight band closing around her mind. *How can it be this way?* she thought.

She went upstairs to her room and returned with some folded

currency which she slipped into Aunt Tanya's pocket. "When I arrived in Orensk, you refused to let me contribute to the food expenses because I was a guest. I'm part of the family now, and with Uncle Vladimer gone for a while and Fyodor's family here, you need extra money. I insist on helping."

"Thank you, Shelly," Aunt Tanya said through tears. "You are right, and I accept it gladly. God bless you, dear."

When Galina finished her tea, she rose to leave. "Would you care to walk part way with me, Shelly?" she asked.

Shelly looked questioningly at Aunt Tanya, who nodded. "You go. It will do you good. For hours you have been sitting here writing."

"I won't be long," Shelly promised.

The snow of the night before had ceased, and Shelly breathed deeply of the crisp, cold air. It *was* good to be out-of-doors.

"Shelly, I've been thinking of the typewriter in Pavel's storeroom. I see no reason why you shouldn't be using it if it is usable."

"Do you think we could get it?"

"The shop is only a few blocks from our home. Would you care to check on it with me tomorrow evening?"

Remembering the horrible trouble Galina's husband was having with the KGB, Shelly said, "I can get along without it. Pytor said he didn't want you to go there."

"I know what he said," Galina answered rather sharply, "but the Scripture copying would go so much faster for you. It might mean extra chapters for someone before you return to America."

"All right, Galina, if you're sure you want to do it."

"I do. Pytor will undoubtedly go out as usual tomorrow evening. You come for supper and we will at least go by the shop and consider it."

Galina turned then, giving Shelly a quick hug, "I'm glad my brother cares about you. He needs someone like you. I'll see you tomorrow."

Turning, Galina walked on, seemingly cheerful, but Shelly sensed the deep undercurrent of worry in her voice.

As she turned to retrace her steps, Shelly noticed a tall, thin man emerge from beside a building. Turning back several times, she saw that he was going the same direction she was.

She had a strange feeling, seeing him still behind her when she entered the Rozkalne house.

Following prayer together, before they went to bed that night,

Aunt Tanya asked, "You will go shopping with me tomorrow, Shelly? We will use some of the money you gave me to try to purchase some extra food to take care of Fyodor's family in case I must be away a while for Vladimer . . ." Her voice trailed off.

Shelly's heart ached for her aunt and she put her arms around the older woman.

"Of course. I want to do whatever I possibly can to assist you in what you have to do."

They returned home late the next afternoon with four net bags bulging. After standing in lines for hours, they had been fortunate to obtain many needed items.

Shelly left for the Shepels' home early that evening. Dusk had fallen but the way had become familiar after walking it several times with Demetri.

It wasn't until she was entering the street to their home that a sense of foreboding enveloped her.

She turned quickly. In the duskiness of the poorly lighted street, she saw a tall, slim figure about a block behind her.

Her heart thumping, Shelly quickened her pace.

She was too frightened to look again until she reached Galina's door.

She looked back as she knocked frantically.

The street seemed clear now. Was it her imagination, or was a tall shadow melting against the house two doors away?

Chapter Fifteen

"Is something wrong?" Galina asked, opening the door. "Your knock sounded so impatient."

"I'm sorry, I guess I'm getting paranoid," Shelly answered with an unsteady laugh.

"What upset you?"

"I thought I was being followed."

A strange clouded look passed over Galina's face before she said, "You must be cold after that walk. I have hot tea ready. I'm glad you came early."

Mrs. Barinov was glad to see Shelly again and hugged her quietly as she took Shelly's coat.

"She said we should do it, although it may cause some problems. She thinks we should stand for our rights as much as possible, especially where it concerns honest, sincere work for the Lord."

"I'm glad she agrees," Shelly said. "I wasn't sure we should try if everyone was against it because the Bible says we should listen to Christian advice and take it into account when making plans."

"By the way," Galina said, "Leonila gave me the books of John and Romans that she had copied. Mamma and Pytor are copying from them now, so we will have copies and can pass one on to others to do the same."

"That's wonderful!" Shelly responded. "But . . . Pytor is helping, too?"

"Yes, why do you seem surprised? He has a fine, clear penmanship, and has time since he hasn't steady work."

Pytor opened the door then, stamping snow from his boots outside before coming into the warm kitchen.

His face lit with a welcoming smile. "Shelly, is good to see you. Demetri was disappointed to leave without telling you, but it is his work."

Pytor looked a bit dejected as he bent to remove his boots, and Shelly remembered that his work papers had been confiscated.

Shrugging out of his heavy coat, he said, "A neighbor needed help with repairing his roof, so God has blessed me with a bit of work, too, today."

He smiled at Shelly, "We must learn patience, difficult as I am finding that to do. Always our God is faithful."

Thinking of what Demetri had told her about Pytor's nightly visits to the KGB, she wondered how he could seem so serene.

But later, when Mrs. Barinov asked if he would be staying home, a sudden cloud seemed to cover his face for a moment.

"No, Mamma," he said quietly.

She didn't question further, and Shelly wondered if she guessed what was happening to this fine man.

Following their supper of sausage with cabbage and potatoes, Pytor pulled on his boots and coat, wound a scarf around his neck to meet his fur hat, and held Galina close for a moment before leaving.

Shelly ducked her head, pretending to pick a piece of lint from her sweater sleeve, not wanting anyone to see the sudden tears in her eyes.

She and Galina left shortly afterward, Mrs. Barinov having insisted on clearing the table and doing the dishes.

"Galina," Shelly asked, "could my being at the print shop cause problems for Aunt Tanya?"

"I do not think so, Shelly. But you need not go with me if you have reservations about it."

"No, I want to get that typewriter if at all possible, but I don't want to cause any extra trouble."

"We will be extra cautious. If there seems any risk at all, we can just wait for another time."

They turned another corner after several blocks, and Galina said, "The lighted building ahead on the right is a small restaurant on the other side of the print shop."

They moved along very slowly, seeming to peruse the displays in the shop windows.

"Galina!" Shelly whispered. "He's there again. The tall, thin man I felt was following me."

Galina let her purse fall to the ground, and bending to retrieve it, scanned the area around them.

"I don't see anyone, but we won't take a chance. Let's go casually into the restaurant."

There were only a few patrons in the room. Shelly and Galina sat at a small round table against the wall where they both had a good view of the entrance and front window.

"This is my treat," Shelly said as they ordered tea and small fruit pastries.

She was taking her first sip of the hot brew when she spotted a movement outside. She whispered over the rim of the glass, "There he is now."

Very casually, Galina lifted her pastry, her glance brushing across to the window. "I see," she said quietly, taking a bite.

When Shelly looked up again, the tall, sparse man was turning from looking in the window and moved back down the street.

"Excuse me a moment," Galina said, standing quickly and heading for the door. She stepped outside and looked down the street in the direction the man had disappeared.

Returning to the table where Shelly sat, Galina smiled and spoke to the proprietor who was watching her curiously.

Sitting down, she grinned, "I told him I found it wasn't snowing after all. By the way, the stranger is evidently going back the way from which we came."

Shelly sighed with relief, "But he was watching us, wasn't he?" she asked quietly.

"Maybe," Galina answered.

They finished their dessert slowly, and strolled unhurriedly out and down the street, glancing briefly at the dark print shop as they passed.

As they paused before the window of a boot shop, Galina said softly, "It looked the same as always, as far as I could see; let's check the back door."

They proceeded part way around the block to a narrow alley. It appeared dark and forbidding to Shelly, but she took Galina's arm and followed her through the snow, glad that Galina knew the way.

The door at which they stopped was barely discernable, but Shelly could vaguely see a boarded-up window on the side of it.

"Vandals smashed the window shortly before the shop was closed," Galina whispered. "Pytor and I covered it."

Carefully she inserted the key in the lock and slowly turned it.

Shelly heard the faint click before Galina turned the knob and pushed the door. It swung open easily and silently.

"Pavel always kept everything well oiled and in good repair," she whispered.

"I surely hope he had time to check the old typewriter," Shelly whispered back.

Instead of going in, Galina softly pulled the door shut and relocked it.

"There are too many people around this time of evening to do any searching," she said, "but I wanted to make sure we could get in."

When they had left the alley and were headed back, Galina said, "I'll walk home with you, so you won't feel afraid. I know you will want to be with your aunt because of her husband's trouble, so we'll go back now."

"But what about the typewriter?" Shelly asked, speaking low because of other pedestrians.

"Perhaps Tanya won't mind if you spend the night at our house tomorrow. You may tell her what we hope to do if you like. Then we'll go about midnight, right after Pytor returns."

"Won't he wonder where you're going?"

"He falls asleep right away; he seems exhausted."

Shelly thought, *It's no wonder, after what he goes through. I'm surprised he doesn't collapse before he gets home.*

Aunt Tanya was very concerned when Shelly told her the next day, fearing for Shelly's safety. But after she assured her Aunt she'd be careful and reminded her of the outcome if they were successful, Aunt Tanya gave her blessing to the venture.

"I'm an accurate, fast typist, Aunt Tanya. I'll be able to accomplish so much more in the little time I have left here. If only I could just ship Bibles to you, but Uncle Vladimer told me it wouldn't be allowed."

"No, dear. They would be confiscated and probably destroyed."

They went to the hidden room for an early supper with Fyodor's family that evening instead of just taking supper down to them.

Ivan and Anna delighted in the finger games Shelly remembered from her childhood and played with them.

When Galina arrived to accompany her to the Shepel home, Shelly went in to say good night to Aunt Natalia.

When she rejoined the others, Shelly said, "She was sleeping. I've not seen her awake very often lately, Aunt Tanya. She looks very fragile, doesn't she?"

Aunt Tanya nodded, "I don't think she will be much longer in this world. Right now, it is a world easy to leave for most of us."

Shelly thought, *The discouragement and sense of fruitlessness steals in even when they're being so brave and wanting to trust the Lord completely.*

Aloud, she said as she hugged her aunt, "I understand, Aunt Tanya. I've learned since coming here how picky my concerns have always been, how shallow compared to the truly important things in life."

At midnight, it was snowing gently but heavily, with no wind blowing when Shelly and Galina left the Shepel home and started through the dark to the dimly lighted business section of Orensk.

"Snow is good," Galina said. "It will cover our tracks tonight in the event anyone notices us while we're out and wonders about the odd hours."

Besides empty string bags on each arm, they both carried an old blanket.

Because the walk was short, they found themselves very quickly at the alley door of the print shop.

Shelly held Galina's blanket while the door was unlocked and they went inside, locking the door behind them.

Shelly could see nothing but a faint glow in the front window from a streetlight on the corner of the block several doors down.

Galina took Shelly's elbow, guiding her across to a door on the left wall. Shelly couldn't see the door, but heard it being unlocked and opened.

Galina guided her through and Shelly heard it close quietly before Galina switched on a small flashlight.

"Demetri gave this to Pytor as a New Year's gift last winter," she said quietly. "Hold it and give me one of the blankets."

Moving a small stool over to the boarded-up window, she proceeded to hang the blanket on nails already around the window area, tucking the fabric in carefully.

Moving her stool to the door, she took the other blanket and covered the door and its frame in the same way.

Taking the flashlight from Shelly, Galina put it in her coat pocket and switched on an overhead light, a bare bulb hung from the ceiling in the small storeroom.

To Shelly there didn't appear to be much of anything they would be able to use. Except for a plain wood table and a straight-backed chair, there were only some shelves holding odds and ends.

Under the lowest shelves, Shelly saw two very large cardboard boxes, both labeled.

"This label says *Clean Rags*, the other *Used Rags*," Galina told her when she asked.

"It looks as though the authorities or vandals may have cleaned out everything important," Shelly said disappointedly.

Galina beckoned to Shelly and together they pulled out the box labeled "Used Rags." Opening the flaps, Galina removed an armful of cloth.

Then bending, she half disappeared inside the huge carton, pushing cloths aside.

When she stood up, she was holding a boxed ream of paper and a folio of carbons.

"Oh, great," Shelly said, taking them. "If we get a typewriter, I could make four or five copies at a time."

"There are about a dozen reams of paper under the cloths," Galina said. "We had been ordering double what we needed every so often those last few months and secreting part of it."

Pulling out another one, Galina handed it to Shelly. "Wrap one in a cloth and put it in your string bag. We'll take a couple of these home for the hand copying.

"With the congregation members each buying a little here and there so as not to attract attention, we can keep producing portions of the Bible slowly but surely."

"Has the typewriter been taken, or is it out in the main room?" Shelly asked.

"We had one out there. I thought we might try bringing it in here. Then if the one with the English keyboard works, we can both type."

Galina dumped the cloths back into the carton, then tucked in the flaps.

"Is there more paper in the other box?" Shelly asked, "or does it really hold just clean rags?"

"The old typewriter," Galina said. "Help me pull the box out from under the shelves."

It scraped on the bare floor as the other one had, and as before, Galina pulled out piles of cloth.

She stood suddenly. "Did you hear something?" she whispered.

"Like what?" Shelly whispered back.

"I'm not sure." Galina tiptoed over to the blanket-covered window, pressing her ear against it.

They both stood absolutely still breathing shallowly, straining to listen.

After what seemed a long time to Shelly, Galina left the window.

"Maybe it was my imagination," she said softly. "Let's see if we can get the typewriter out of the box."

Together they bent over the carton on opposite sides, lifting out the heavy, awkward ball of what looked like coat fabric.

They lugged it to the little table and Galina unfolded the thick wool covering, revealing an ancient upright Royal typewriter.

"May I try it?" Shelly asked. "Your brother must have worked on it; it looks so clean."

Galina tore a length of paper from a remnant roll of newsprint on the shelf and Shelly inserted it into the machine. Her fingers flicked over the keyboard: *The quick brown fox jumped over the sleeping dog.*

"The old typewriters were certainly noisy," Galina said. "It will need a cushioning under it if we work here. But at least it seems to be in working order."

"My shoulder bag has a foam insert in one side," Shelly said. "It's not very thick, but it should help a little. I'll bring it."

"Shelly, are you absolutely sure you want to do this typewriting?"

"Yes."

"All right, then; let's put this on that end of the table, and I'll see if Pavel's typewriter is still here."

Snapping the wall switch off, Galina loosened one edge of the protective blanket and opened the door.

Through the front window across the large darkened room, they saw in the swirling snow the figures of a couple slowly strolling by, arm in arm.

"I guess it *would* be very difficult for us to try to carry the heavy thing to your home or Aunt Tanya's, wouldn't it?" Shelly whispered. "Without being noticed, I mean."

"I'm afraid we would be unable to, Shelly, even at night. Then we might be accused of stealing something the authorities had taken into their jurisdiction."

From the storeroom door Shelly watched Galina's dark shadow move surely along the edge of the room to a dark shape that looked like it might be a large desk.

In a few moments, Shelly heard a whispered, "It's here!" She went to where Galina was gathering the typewriter up into her arms.

"There is a chair on the other side of the desk," Galina said softly. "It's on casters. Will you please roll it after me?"

"Okay," Shelly whispered, feeling her way around the piece of furniture until she felt the back of the chair.

She pulled it out from the kneehole of the desk and started to turn it toward the storeroom.

But it swiveled too easily, suddenly rolling ahead, whacking into the desk and knocking Shelly to her knees.

Galina turned quickly, glancing apprehensively toward the front window. "What's wrong?"

"You were right about Pavel keeping things well oiled," Shelly whispered back. "Do you think anyone heard that?"

"I guess not; I hope not."

Shelly stayed where she was, listening, then got up and pushed the chair after Galina into the storeroom.

Closing the door behind her, she switched on the light and quickly fixed the blanket over the nails above the door frame as Galina had earlier.

"This will work fine," Galina said as Shelly guided the chair to the table where she was putting Pavel's typewriter. "With both of us typing, we can accomplish much."

"Shall we start right now?" Shelly asked.

"I thought it would be best to get everything set up tonight and bring something to quiet the machines as much as possible. If all seems to be going well, we'll start tomorrow."

Galina brought another ream of paper from the depths of the rags box and placed it on the table between the two typewriters.

"There's a wide shallow drawer under the table top on the side nearest the wall," she said, shoving the big box back under the overhanging shelves.

"We'll keep it open while we type and each use half of it for our copy as we type it. In the event anyone comes, we can quickly conceal our work.

"You think of everything," Shelly said.

"I've learned to plan ahead defensively," Galina said. "If you will take both the string bags, I'll turn the light off and use the door blanket to cover the table."

When they had locked the storeroom door, they crept slowly through the darkness to the outer door.

Unlocking it, Galina looked out into the alley. All seemed quiet.

"The snow has already covered our tracks," Shelly whispered.

After Galina locked the door, she took her bag from Shelly and they both snugged their mufflers around their necks and over their hoods.

"A light just went on in that high window next door," Shelly whispered as they headed down the alley toward the nearest street.

"It's the restaurant kitchen," Galina whispered. "They must be starting the bread and pastries for the day already. We'll have to remember that."

The bag of paper was heavy on Shelly's arm by the time they reached Galina's home. It reminded Shelly of the morning she and Demetri carried Bibles and hymnals from the trash dump.

A cot had been prepared in Mrs. Barinov's room for Shelly. She fell asleep almost immediately, wondering whether Demetri had slept there as a little boy.

Later that morning, Shelly carried the paper to Aunt Tanya's home for Fyodor and Leonila, after making plans for that evening with Galina. They decided it might be best to go while Pytor was away, and before the village got so quiet every unusual noise would be noticed, so at seven o'clock Galina stopped by for her.

They came to the alley from a different street than before and quietly entered the back door of the print shop.

As they moved across the dusky room, they heard an occasional sound from the restaurant next door.

"I'm glad the storeroom is on the opposite side of the shop," Galina whispered. "The pharmacy on that side closes early."

As soon as they were in the storeroom with the door covered and the light on, Shelly settled in the chair before her typewriter and giggled, "This is the first time I've typed bundled up like a teddy bear."

"We would be much too cold without our boots and coats," Galina said. "There is no way to heat this little room except by leaving the door open and lighting the heaters in the other room.

When your hands start getting too cold, put a couple of these on," she added, dropping some heavy socks on the table.

Picking one up, she slipped it on her hand, poking her fingers through conveniently cut slits. "This way our fingers are free to type but our hands will keep fairly warm."

"That's a great idea, like golf gloves," Shelly said. "I hope these aren't Pytor's socks you've cut," she added mischievously.

"No, some badly worn ones of Pavel's. I'll darn them like new before he returns."

Galina sat down and removed the cover of her typewriter while Shelly inserted paper and carbons in hers and opened her little Testament in readiness to start typing.

"Oh, dear," Galina said.

"What's wrong?" Shelly asked.

"There's no ribbon in my typewriter. I can't understand why it would have been removed."

"Perhaps Pavel was preparing to change it when he was arrested," Shelly suggested.

"That's the only logical reason unless the KGB removed it just to frustrate us when Pavel is back in business again. God willing, that he is eventually released.

"I think our only extra ones are kept at home except for one we had on this shelf."

Galina moved the stool to the shelves and climbed up to feel around on the highest one.

"Nothing," she said, getting down. "I'm going to search the desk area in the other room."

"Aren't you afraid someone will see your light?" Shelly asked.

"I won't use one. I'm familiar enough with that old desk to check it in the dark."

"I'll have to turn this one off while I go through the door," she said.

"That's okay," Shelly said. "Just leave it open; I'll quit typing. Can I help you?"

"No, I'll be back in a minute."

When she returned and had switched the light back on, she said, "You must have guessed correctly about Pavel starting to change this. Look what I found under the desk."

Shelly saw in Galina's hand a tangled, dusty mass of ribbon. "Doesn't look very usable, does it?" she said.

"If I don't have extras at home, I'll have to try to clean this some way and rewind it until I can have Demetri get me one when he's in Leningrad.

"Would you mind, Shelly, if I went right now? If I don't, I won't get any work done at all tonight."

"I don't mind. You go ahead."

Galina rebundled her scarf around her neck and stepped to the door.

"Rehang the blanket when I leave. I'll lock just the outer door."

As soon as Galina had left, Shelly settled down at her typewriter, feeling bulky and awkward in her heavy coat but glad that she had it on and had stuffed her warm slacks into her boot tops.

Propping her Testament open with a corner of the typing paper box, she began,

Matthew . . . Chapter 1 . . . The book of the generation of Jesus Christ . . .

"Even with padding under it, this old machine sure is noisy," she said half-aloud.

Then, as she typed, she became engrossed in the age-old story enfolding on the paper, and she was glad she was providing for people who didn't have copies of God's Word.

Shelly's fingers flew nimbly over the keys with a steady rhythmic clacking, except when she paused to insert new packets of paper and carbons, dropping the typed ones into the open drawer.

She didn't hear the noises at the alley door of the print shop or the clomp of heavy boots across the floor of the adjoining room.

Chapter Sixteen

It happened so swiftly Shelly wondered later how she was able to keep her wits about her.

The door burst open, ripping the blanket from the nails as an armed uniformed man filled the doorway of the little room.

Over his shoulder, she saw another man pressing forward.

In one steady movement, Shelly stood, partially turning to conceal her hand closing the drawer and slipping the Testament into her pocket.

Although her eyes were wide with fear, and her heart beat wildly, she felt calm inside.

"Show me what to do, Lord," she prayed silently.

The man stepped forward, snapping a question at her, but she couldn't understand him.

While he yelled at her and she wondered frantically whether to tell him she was American, a quiet voice seemed to speak inside her thoughts from a verse she had copied a few days earlier: *When you are arrested, don't worry about what to say . . .*

The man still at the doorway strode to the typewriter and ripped out the sheet of paper, leaving a torn portion in the machine. He glanced at it a moment, then shoved it in his overcoat pocket.

Grabbing Shelly's arm, he propelled her out the door and across the shop to the open alley door, with the armed man following close behind.

One on either side of her, they marched her down the alley to where a black car stood waiting.

Shoving her into the backseat, the armed man climbed in beside her while the other one slid behind the steering wheel.

As they pulled away from the curb, Shelly saw a tall, thin figure step from the shadows and stand watching while they drove away.

Shelly wondered if they were taking her to the KGB headquarters where Pytor went every night, and where they had taken Uncle Vladimer.

Her heart pounded frantically at the thought and nausea began rising with what might be before her.

But the car was turning toward the edge of town and even in the dusk of early night, Shelly recognized the mounds of the trash dump as they passed and swung onto the main road.

She wondered what Galina would think when she returned and found her gone, the doors standing open.

"And Demetri—will I be released by the time he returns?" Shelly pondered these things, trying to persuade herself she would be released as soon as they discovered who she was.

After what seemed less than half an hour, the car plowed through the snow before the gate in a high stone wall.

The driver pressed the horn, and immediately a searchlight from one of the towers on the wall shone on them. The gate opened and they drove through.

She was hustled across a courtyard and through a heavy door into a bleak hall where she was turned over to two other guards.

These two, both much younger than the others, were armed only with flashlights and blunt clubs protruding from their back pockets.

She was escorted down several halls and damp stairways, then into a tiny empty cell.

One of the young men opened the narrow door which had a small barred window, and motioned her inside.

As the door thudded behind her, she heard the clang of a bolt and found herself in utter darkness, except for a tiny bulb on the wall above the door, its light too dim to offer any illumination.

Shelly stood uncertainly just inside the door, recalling the location of the items in the closet-sized cell that had been briefly exposed by the guard's light.

Along the right wall was a cot with a thin mattress, a rickety stool, and in one corner a cracked clay pot which she assumed was her toilet.

Forlornly she crossed the few feet to the cot and sat down, huddling in fear and loneliness.

"I'm completely cut off from the outside world," she mumbled, feeling more forsaken than ever before in her life.

Doubts began to gnaw at her. Was God really aware she was here. Did He truly care?

"Maybe no one will ever find out where I am," she whispered to herself, remembering how reluctant the police had been to tell Aunt Tanya anything about Uncle Vladimer.

"And she will be frantic about what has happened to me," Shelly said aloud. "How could I do this to her? How could they do this to me?"

Shelly felt nervous and distraught, her mind beginning to dart from thought to thought so that she couldn't even seem to pray except to say over and over, "What can I do? Show me what to do."

She stood up and began pacing slowly in the small space, her hand out to keep from bumping the wall, using the tiny lightbulb as her guide.

After a while, her scraping steps seemed to be keeping time with a tune that was filtering through her worries.

Why should I feel discouraged,
. . . .
His eye is on the sparrow,
And I know He watches me;

And from somewhere deep in her memory arose part of a verse:

Are not two sparrows sold for a farthing? And one of them shall not fall on the ground without your Father.

Tears suddenly welled in Shelly's eyes and her heart cried out to God to help her endure whatever was ahead.

She had no idea what time it was. She couldn't see her watch, but she realized she was very tired.

Finding the cot, she lay down, keeping her coat and scarf on for warmth. The rough mattress made rustling sounds when she stretched out. She decided it must contain straw or leaves.

Shelly was just beginning to drowse when she felt something move across her neck, then her face. At the same time, before she could react, she felt a crawling sensation at the neckline and sleeves of her sweater.

"Bedbugs!" she screamed aloud, jumping up and trying to get the things off her. She had heard of them and her senses were repulsed as she worked frantically to free herself of them.

Feeling the stool against her leg, she sank down on it. It swayed precariously.

Sobbing, she brushed at the areas of her body that still felt crawly, glad her boot tops were tight around the legs of her slacks.

She was thankful, too, that Galina had suggested she fasten a scarf snugly around her head for extra warmth, because it had evidently kept the creatures from her hair.

Realizing she was getting very cold, she shrugged deeper into her coat, pulling the hood over her head.

"What if I had fallen asleep before they came out?" she thought. "Ugh!" Shelly shuddered, sleep having fled for now.

But drowsiness began to overtake her again after a while, and she huddled on the stool half asleep until hours later when a noise at the door awakened her completely.

She realized it was morning and her body was badly cramped from her odd sitting position on the rickety stool.

Shelly stood up, noticing the barred, dirty window high in the wall through which the early morning light was filtering.

When she turned, she saw on the floor before the door a cup and small bowl that had been pushed through a slot in the bottom of the door.

The metal cup held tea, weak but hot. She saw in the bowl about two spoonfuls of some sort of porridge.

The hot cup was comforting to her fingers, still protruding from the holes in Pavel's socks. But as she lifted the cup to her mouth, she saw small red spots covering her fingers. Her face felt as though the bites were there, too.

I guess the bugs won after all, she thought.

She ate the few bites of cereal, deciding it was made from oatmeal, wishing it had a bit of salt and sugar in it and some milk.

She scraped the bottom of the little wood bowl with the spoon to get every bit, thinking of bacon and eggs, hotcakes with syrup, hot cereal with a generous pat of butter melting in the middle.

As she stooped to put the utensils back on the floor where she had found them, she wondered if this was what cousin Valentina was having for breakfast, and how many such morning meals Pavel had eaten during his years in prison.

"Thank you, Lord," she whispered, "for what I've just eaten. I didn't mean to seem ungrateful by thinking of more ample delicious meals."

She wondered what she should do now to use the time during

the day ahead, in case they didn't release her to go back to Orensk.

She did a few stretching exercises to loosen up her tenseness and ran in place, humming the tune of the night before: "His eye is on the sparrow, and I know He cares for me."

Shelly stopped suddenly, remembering the Testament in her coat. She reached into the pocket, thankful she hadn't been searched.

Enough daylight was beginning to enter the cell now through the little window so she could read.

She settled down on the low stool and thumbed through the pages of the little book, reading Scriptures along the way that she had underlined at various times.

When she had gone through all the books, she reopened at the card with Aunt Tanya's address that she had been using as a book-mark and decided to read consecutively.

I beseech you, therefore, brethren, that you present your bodies a living sacrifice, holy, acceptable unto God, which is your reasonable service. And be not conformed to this world: but . . .

The cell-door bolt slid back and the door opened in one noisy movement.

Shelly jumped up, startled and frightened, to face a uniformed man about Demetri's age, holding a small club.

He said something Shelly didn't understand, then noticing the book, held out his hand.

When she didn't move, he stepped forward and snatched it from her.

He studied it for a moment, then asked, "You speak English?"

"Yes," Shelly answered with relief, hoping she might find help from this young man. "I'm an American. I shouldn't be in here."

But he said roughly, "Come with me," shoving the book in his pocket so he could grasp her arm and propel her out the door.

When they started down the corridor, he released his grip and strode along beside her.

"Where are you taking me?" Shelly asked, her voice quaver-ing.

"Interrogation."

They walked in silence, their boots the only sound as they passed door after metal door on either side of the corridors.

Shelly wondered fleetingly about the people behind those doors, and became increasingly apprehensive about her destination.

After climbing two stairways, they entered a more well-kept hall with panelled doors instead of cells.

She was ushered into a beautifully furnished office with a carpeted floor. Behind a well-polished desk stood a middle-aged man, his features almost handsome.

The guard spoke from just behind her, repeating in English, "Prisoner from Entering-Cell 1403. This is Comrade Varonyuk."

Shelly heard the door close as the man behind the desk stood, gesturing to a chair nearby. "You speak only English? I am Victor Varonyuk. Please sit down."

Every fiber of Shelly's being wanted to be able to trust the effusive friendliness this man displayed. But as she stepped forward, she sensed the hardness and cruelty lurking in the depths of his steel-blue eyes.

She sat down in the designated chair next to the desk. "I am an American. May I please ask why I've been brought here?"

"The prisoner does not ask the questions," he said, the smile leaving his lean face.

Slowly he sat down, carefully placing his elbows on the desk and methodically placing his fingertips together.

"What is your name?"

"Shelly Lee."

"You were trespassing, Shelly Lee."

"But that office belongs to a friend of mine. I had permission to be there. I wasn't trespassing."

Varonyuk's hands formed fists which he slammed down on the desk top.

"Silence! For now it is government property! You were trespassing on government property!"

Shelly jumped, startled by his sudden outburst and the change in him.

"I'm sorry," she said meekly.

"Also, you were proliferating dangerous propaganda," Varonyuk said, his voice controlled.

"Propaganda?"

"Propaganda against the great Soviet government," he said, shoving toward her a piece of paper she recognized immediately as the one torn from her typewriter.

Softly she read aloud, "The generation of Jesus Christ," adding, "The Son of the living God."

"Hah!" Varonyuk spat. "Have you not heard what a former

Chairman of the Leningrad Soviet said? 'We will grapple with the Lord God in due season. We shall vanquish him in his highest heaven.' "

An ugly, twisted smile slid across Victor Varonyuk's face as he finished the quote.

Looking directly into the man's eyes, almost unaware that she was speaking, Shelly said very quietly, "Then why are you so afraid concerning my writing about Him?"

The man's inner being seemed to explode with vicious anger. Jumping to his feet, he shouted a command. Instantly the door opened.

Shelly was terribly frightened; the enraged Communist seemed about to strike her. But he gripped the edge of the desk, his arms trembling, his teeth clenched.

As the young guard's stubby club prodded her across the room and out the door, Varonyuk's words followed her, "God, is it? We will see! Cell 48! Cell 48! Rot there if you must!"

The guard led Shelly back along the corridors and stairways through which they had come earlier.

Eventually they approached the open cell where she had spent the previous night, but he took her past it and down to an even lower floor, damp and musty smelling.

He pushed her roughly past the cells and down another, narrower corridor which ended in a steep flight of narrow stairs going almost straight down.

Shelly descended the steep steps into the cold, damp darkness, her only light the guard's flashlight.

She stood at the bottom of the steps while the guard came down.

Shelly had a quick thought of grabbing his legs and throwing him off balance, then trying to get away. But she knew that was hopeless; where could she run to?

The guard grasped her arm, leading her along a narrow walkway to a cell door. He opened it and shoved her inside.

She heard his footsteps leaving and climbing back up the stairs.

Deathly quiet surrounded her. It was so black she couldn't see her hand when she held it up in front of her face.

Feeling like a blind person, she groped around the cell, finding only a tin cup on the bare board bunk and nearby a crock on the floor. Nothing else.

Remembering that she had read of communication between prisoners by tapping on the walls in code, Shelly picked up the cup and tapped it against the wall, hoping with all her heart that she would hear a tap in return.

But there was no reply. She tried again and again with various sequences of tapping. Was she the only person down in this place?

She felt the wall with her hand; it was wet with moisture running down.

Remembering Varonyuk's parting shout and surrounded by the pervading darkness and the terrible quiet, Shelly felt abject terror growing within her. She felt as if she might begin screaming uncontrollably.

Tears filled her eyes and slipped down her cheeks. She had felt alone the night before, but it was nothing compared to the desolateness and utter despair that filled her now.

"Where are you, Lord?" she cried aloud.

As she stood there, sobbing, the quiet seemed to take on a new dimension. For some strange reason, she recalled a passage read by her pastor several years ago:

> A great and strong wind rent the mountains, and broke in pieces the rocks before the Lord; but the Lord was not in the wind: and after the wind, an earthquake; but the Lord was not in the earthquake: And after the earthquake, a fire; but the Lord was not in the fire: And after the fire a still small voice.

She moved to the plank cot and sat on its edge, glad there was no mattress to harbor the terror and discomfort of the previous night.

Her thoughts wandered to her happy childhood, to memories of her parents and Gram.

She lingered longest on thoughts of, and prayer for, Demetri. Demetri, whom she might never see again, who would never know what had happened to her.

The weariness of worry and fear, then of resignation, hunched her lower on the wood plank.

She pulled her legs up on the makeshift cot and lay down with her knees pulled up against her chest. Folding her arms across her shoulders as best she could to stop the shivering, she prayed. "God, I know there is no place on earth that can hide me from you. Even down here, I am sure you are with me. Forgive my doubts. Give me strength for whatever you want me to do."

She slept then.

When Shelly awoke, she was cold and hungry and had lost track of time in the darkness. She felt suspended somewhere in space.

"Is it the same day, I wonder," she said aloud, startling herself with her own voice. "Or is it tomorrow already? Or have I been here only a few hours? Or days?"

Such thoughts brought a special terror and she fought the fear that she might not be able to retain her sanity.

"Stop that!" she said, as though speaking to another person. "Think of something to do to occupy yourself."

She forced herself to recite poetry she had learned long ago: multiplication tables, hymns, ditties from her childhood autograph book.

On a hill far away stood an old rugged cross,
The emblem of suffering and shame. . . .[1]

For God so loved the world, that he gave his only begotten Son, that whosoever believeth in him should not perish, but have everlasting life.

Silent night, holy night,
All is calm, all is bright. . . .

Abou BenAdhem, may his tribe increase;
Awoke one night from a deep dream of peace,
And saw within the moonlight in his room,
An angel writing in a book of gold. . . .[2]

I pledge allegiance to the flag
of the United States of America,
And to the republic for which it stands. . . .

"Had an hour gone by yet," Shelly wondered aloud. "Several, perhaps? ten minutes?

Twelve times two is twenty-four;
Twelve times three is thirty-six. . . .

She kept on and on, wishing she had something to eat or drink.

---

[1] *The Old Rugged Cross.* Copyright 1913 by George Bennard. © renewed 1941 (extended). The Rodeheaver Co., owner. Used by permission.
[2] From *Rubaiyat of Omar Kjayyam.*

Roses are red, violets are blue
I think you're great, what about you?

Reciting, singing, napping . . . reciting, singing, napping.

Putting a hand against the wall to orient herself, she ran in place until she was exhausted, then lay down on the board to think and finally, again to sleep.

When she awoke, she prayed, then started again:

Seven times two is fourteen,
Seven times three is twenty-one. . . .

Praise Him! Praise Him!
Jesus, our blessed Redeemer!
For our sins
He suffered. . . .

Two hundred divided by ten is twenty

Four score and seven years ago,
Our fathers brought forth on this continent, . . .

Then she heard a sound. In the vast stillness, a sound other than her own voice.

Shelly listened. Yes, it was footsteps, then the sliding of a heavy bolt. The door opened.

The flashlight blinded her. She scrunched her eyes shut, putting her sock-clad hands over them.

"I'm sorry, Shelly," a male voice said. "Your eyes will be all right in a moment. Here."

Shelly opened her eyes very slowly, afraid she was hallucinating. The guard pointed his flashlight toward a corner to help her eyes adjust. As her eyes focused, she saw the harshness of the small cell.

The voice belonged to the young guard who had brought her here. He was holding a metal cup out to her.

"Thank you," Shelly said, reaching for it, tears filling her eyes. She put it to her lips, dry from reciting.

It contained tea, hot and sugared.

The guard reached in his pocket. "You were not to have anything. Cell 48 means strict solitary with no food or drink."

He handed her a chunk of dark bread and a piece of cheese.

"Then why did you bring this?" Shelly asked, taking a deep whiff of the tangy bread aroma.

"I had to. It is part of my meal. I could not eat today, knowing you were here without anything."

"How long have I been in here?"

"Two nights and a day. Also, part of today."

"What time of day is it?"

"It is the noon hour. I must go now, or it may be discovered I am here. Finish the tea, so I may return the cup."

Shelly drank the last sweet, warm swallow of the comforting liquid. Handing the cup to him, she said, "You called me Shelly when you came in. How did you know?"

Before he took the cup, he smiled gently and reached into his pocket. He handed her a small book. "Your name is in here."

It was her Testament.

"Oh, thank you!" she said gratefully.

"Shelly," he said, hesitantly, "my name is Nicoli. May I please keep the book another day . . . please?"

"Yes," Shelly said, surprised. "Of course. I can't read in here anyway." Then remembering, she asked quickly, "You're not going to destroy it?"

"No, Shelly," he said slowly, very seriously. "I will take close care of it."

She handed the Testament back to him, and as he turned to go, she asked, "Do you know how long I'll be here?"

"No, I do not. Try to not dwell on it."

The door closed behind him, and the light disappeared as his footsteps faded away.

Shelly couldn't stop the tears that slid down her cheeks.

"I'm glad *you* know how long I'll be here, God," she whispered. "I'm very frightened. Help me to keep up my courage, trusting You to know what's best. And thank you for the food, for Nicoli's kindness."

Minutes slid into hours again, the dark silence pressing against her.

Holy, holy, holy! Lord God, Almighty!
Early in the morning, our song shall rise to Thee;

Thirteen multiplied by three is thirty-nine.
Thirteen multiplied by five is . . . sixty-five.

Mary had a little lamb
Its fleece was white as snow,
And everywhere that Mary went—

A sound! The door!

Shelly turned to the grating bolt, her heart thankful that the friendly Nicoli was returning.

But it wasn't Nicoli behind the glaring flashlight. Two burly uniformed men stood there.

"Come with us immediately!"

Chapter Seventeen

Each of them gripping one of her arms, they propelled her out of the cell and down the hall to the stairs leading upward.

Her heart pounding, Shelly's only deduction was that she was being taken to an experience like that of Pytor's.

Could she possibly survive a beating without revealing anything they would ask her to?

Shelly's legs seemed devoid of strength. She was shoved and partly dragged through the cell-lined corridors.

She was shocked when at the top of some steps, she was shoved through a door into a carpeted hall.

Were they taking her to Victor Varonyuk again? With dread she remembered his parting shout about letting her rot in that cell below ground. What was he going to do to her now? Or was someone else to finish Varonyuk's threat?

They paused before a panelled door. One of the guards knocked smartly, opened the door and snapped, "Prisoner from Cell 48."

Shelly was shoved so forcefully through the door that she stumbled forward, sprawling on the lush carpet.

She saw the heavy, shiny black boots approaching across the carpet as she struggled to rise.

A large lean hand reached down. Above it Varonyuk's voice spoke, as smooth and friendly as the moments when they had first met.

"They are rough fellows, are they not?" he said, taking her sock-clad hand and helping her up.

Guiding her to the chair beside his desk, he strode to a position behind the large desk.

"You did not give me your name when we met."

"My name is Shelly Lee. I did give it to you last time, and I am an American."

Ignoring her comment, he said, "I assume you have learned your lesson since you were here three days ago, Miss Shelly Lee?"

She stared at him, wondering how to answer.

His voice began to lose its smoothness. "Are you ready now to confess your crimes?"

"I've committed no crimes," Shelly said quietly.

"You must criticize your crimes," Victor Varonyuk said, stepping around the desk toward her.

"It will go much easier for you when you confess. The Soviet government is lenient. We feel you are a good young woman, but you must conform to us."

"But I'm an American," Shelly stressed adamantly. "I haven't done anything against your government."

A hardness settled over Varonyuk's face, his eyes narrowed. "Tell me about your spy activities."

"My what!" Shelly exclaimed, taken by surprise at the absurd questioning. "I'm no spy. I'm in your country visiting my relatives."

The man's long arm swung forward, his hand hitting Shelly's cheek sharply.

"Who do you send your reports to?"

"But I don't—" Shelly began.

Varonyuk gave her a blow to the side of her head as he shouted, "You will tell me how you spied for your government!"

Hunched in the chair, her ear ringing, Shelly said nothing.

She heard the door opening and closing and she pictured the guards coming for her again. She would be glad to get out of here. The cell was almost better than Varonyuk's anger and what he might do to her.

But when Shelly looked around, she found herself alone.

She sat alert, her nerves tense, waiting for them to come for her. No one came.

In a daze, Shelly watched the clock on the wall. The second hand slowly made its rounds, over and over and over. The hour hand moved methodically from six to seven, then eight and nine.

At nine-thirty, she heard the door open. Footsteps approached, muffled in the deep carpet.

Deeply apprehensive, Shelly waited, not turning.

The boots and uniform pants that passed her chair looked like Varonyuk's, but the voice that spoke to her was deeper than his.

Shelly looked up at the man who stood before her.

Patches of white at the temples and sideburns brightened the thick brown hair surrounding a bald area over the heavy, round face. Lines radiated from the corners of the deep, squinty eyes and down along the sides of his mouth as he said cordially, "Thank you for waiting. We have had your confessions typed. I've brought them for you to sign."

"I've confessed to nothing. I've done nothing," Shelly stated, her voice breaking. Instinctively, she ducked, expecting his hand against her head.

"I, Boris Gula, am a patient man, Miss Lee. If you do not sign today, you will tomorrow or next week, or next year. But you will confess to your crimes against the Soviet government."

Shelly glanced at the paper he held out to her.

"But I can't read Russian. I wouldn't even know what I was signing."

"Ah, of course. Shall I read it to you?"

Shelly shook her head. "I've not committed any crime."

Very slowly, Boris Gula put the papers on the desk. He stood a moment, "Tomorrow then," he said, and left the room.

Immediately one of the guards who had brought her there hours before entered and roughly escorted her back through the maze of stairs and tunnels to a cell with an outside window covered with bars, and occupied cells on either side.

After the door clanged shut, Shelly stood in the center of the cell, not wanting to go near the mattressed cot the guard's light had revealed.

Eventually her fatigue overcame her. Moving forward in the dark until her leg contacted the edge of the cot, she reached down, shuddering with distaste, and pulled the mattress to the floor. With her foot she shoved it under the plank cot fastened to the wall. Hoping none of the creatures were there, she gingerly sat down.

Huddled there, she watched the stars through the bars of the small window until they disappeared in the blur of early dawn. She thought she was praying, but her befuddled mind wasn't sure. Then, unable to resist the sleep overtaking her, she stretched out on the plank.

Shelly awoke to find sunshine slanting across the littered cell floor. She felt cold, grimy, and very hungry. She wondered if they would give her anything today.

She listened with anticipation a short while later, hearing footsteps in the corridor, door slots opening and metal objects being slid over the floor.

She watched the slot beneath the door. The sounds came closer and now were at the next cell.

A metal cup and wooden bowl appeared in the slot, and Shelly rushed forward to pick them up.

Bringing them to the plank, she forgot the stench of the cell for a few moments as she held the cup to her lips, inhaling the steamy aroma of the weak tea.

The few spoonfuls of corn mush seemed the most delicious food she had ever tasted. Shelly relished every tiny grain clinging to the bowl. She knew her thanksgiving to God for this food was the most sincere she had ever uttered over any meal.

After she had replaced the utensils, she tidied herself as best she could. It was while doing this that she noticed the markings on the walls. Investigating, she found scratched into the surface many phrases and lines she could not read.

Studying the other scratchings and a few pencil markings, she suddenly gasped, smiling to herself, "Of course, that's what I'll do. It may encourage someone else; it surely will help pass some time."

As she mused aloud, her hands searched her coat pockets.

Pulling out a felt-tip pen, she reached out to the wall and began to print.

> *God will never leave me*
> *or forsake me.*
> *The wages of sin is death;*
> *but the gift of God is eternal life.*
> *Serve the Lord with gladness:*
> *come before his presence with singing.*

Wiping the grime away first with her sock-covered hand, on and on Shelly wrote, the pen moving easily across the concrete walls.

> *Know ye that the Lord, he is God:*
> *it is he that has made us.*
> *I had fainted, unless I had believed*
> *to see the goodness of the Lord*
> *in the land of the living.*

Hours passed. Hunger had been pulling at her stomach for quite a while when the little bowl was pushed through the slot.

Shelly picked it up eagerly, ignoring her soiled hands.

The half-filled bowl of lukewarm liquid smelled faintly of overcooked, rotting cabbage, but she sipped it anyway until the bowl was empty.

Shelly had just replaced the bowl on the floor in front of the slot when the bolt clanged, the door opened, and a heavy boot banged the bowl aside as a guard entered.

Motioning to her to precede him, he took her through the corridors and stairs to the office where she had been interrogated previously. Her heart began to pound, her throat became dry. She feared what she might be going to face this time.

It was Victor Varonyuk seated behind the desk. His face inscrutable, he motioned her to the chair beside the desk.

Shelly noticed as she sat down that she was in easy reach of his arm. She tried unobtrusively to push the chair back away from him, but it wouldn't move on the heavy rug.

"I am surprised," he said, "that you have not yet signed your confession. It is possible that you could have been home by now had you done so."

The smile on his face was worse than no smile at all. The latent cruelty Shelly saw behind it frightened her.

She answered nothing, remembering his response the last time she had affirmed her innocence to him.

His voice was controlled as he said, "Miss Lee, you are trying my patience. You will sign this now." He put a pen beside the typed page.

It would be so easy to sign it, Shelly thought. But what would happen to Aunt Tanya if it was said that she had harbored a spy? And what about Demetri? What would he think? Surely he wouldn't believe it, but would his aquaintance with her cause him trouble?

She was startled from her thoughts by Varonyuk's harsh command. "I said, sign this! Now!"

"I cannot sign. It isn't true."

His hand flashed forward with such speed she barely perceived the movement before it smacked against her face.

Shelly's breath drew in, then out in a cry of pain.

She felt sudden tears mingling with blood from her nose and the side of her mouth.

Varonyuk's face was contorted with rage, his arm back, ready to swing again.

Shelly avoided the blow by sliding off the chair onto her knees, her face hidden on her crossed arms as she hit the floor.

"How dare you!" Varonyuk said, his voice low, menacing. Then its pitch rose, "How dare you not conform! How dare you defy me!"

Varonyuk's heavy boot smashed against Shelly's shoulder, glancing off onto the side of her head.

Her next memory was of being dragged along a corridor by a guard on each side gripping her arm.

She heard a bolt and the scrape of heavy hinges. She was shoved forward, landing on her hands and knees.

The door clanged shut.

Then someone was gently helping her to her feet.

Raising her head, Shelly looked dazedly around into the concerned faces of a dozen women.

She couldn't understand their words, but the murmurs of comfort communicated their compassion.

Helping her to the bottom one of a tier of bunks, one of them, a motherly woman, dabbed at Shelly's face with a bit of cloth she'd moistened in the last of a cup of tea.

Shelly winced and tried to smile her thanks through swollen lips.

They helped her lie down and then spread a blanket over her. Her head throbbed, her eyes closed, and she slept.

A hand gently shaking her shoulder woke her. It was early evening.

Gentle arms assisted her in sitting up. A cup was held to her sore lips, and she took deep gulps of warm tea.

"Thank you," Shelly said. "Do any of you speak English?"

A girl about her own age, sitting on a bunk across from her, spoke up, "Yes, I do. What is your name?"

"I'm Shelly Lee, an American," she answered, taking the bowl and chunk of bread offered by the older woman next to her.

Shelly noticed that all the other women were eating.

"Did she give me her supper?" Shelly asked the girl, nodding toward the elder one beside her.

"No. We told the guard there was an extra prisoner in here." She smiled. "But Lyda washed your face with her tea earlier," she added.

"Thank you, Lyda," Shelly said to the woman next to her. Then knowing she didn't understand the words, she put her arm around the thin, shawl-wrapped shoulders, giving her a hug.

Lyda shyly returned the hug, smiling in the dimness.

"I'm Nina," the girl said. "I'll introduce the rest of us in the morning."

Shelly nodded. "They arrested me for copying the Bible. Is that why all of you are here?"

"Only Lyda," Nina answered. Then she gave a short laugh. "Most of us are accused of a lot of petty crimes, or what the KGB calls crimes. Two of us, well, we deserve to be here."

Shelly glanced around, wondering who was responsible for what crimes. Then she realized it really didn't matter. It was good to not be alone. And she was very glad Lyda was here, someone else who believed in God.

In the next few days, Shelly discovered that Lyda had been witnessing to the women about the Lord.

Now, with Nina interpreting for her, Shelly with Lyda began a simple Bible study . . . without a Bible.

But much of God's Word was deep in both their hearts, and they recalled portions that fit the discussions each evening.

During the day, the women filed out to a brightly lighted room where they sewed military uniforms assembly-line fashion on heavy-duty sewing machines.

When they returned to the cell in time for the evening serving of thin soup, bread and tea, they all seemed eager to hear what Shelly and Lyda had to say about the subjects they brought up.

Even the hardest of the women had questions concerning the God they had been taught to believe didn't exist. Many of the women had tears in their eyes as the evenings progressed.

Lost in the routine of little food and long work hours, Shelly stopped counting the days.

The terror of another call to Varonyuk's office faded. She hoped he had decided to leave her alone.

But another, greater fear began to press her mind. Perhaps they would leave her here forever.

She spoke of the possibility of getting word out to Aunt Tanya or the American Embassy, but the women's responses about their experiences with correspondence discouraged her from trying.

Then one day, shortly after they had returned to the cell after work, it happened.

Shelly had just taken her first sip of tea when the door clanged open. The guard standing in the door snapped, "Prisoner Lee, come with me; immediately! Comrade Varonyuk has sent for you."

Chapter Eighteen

Her heart quaking, Shelly left the cell amid the murmurs of concern from the other women.

But the guard didn't take her directly to Varonyuk's office. Instead, he escorted her to a unit Shelly had not been allowed to visit more than one time since her arrest.

A heavy-set woman in a guard's uniform monitered the showers and pointed Shelly to one.

How good the water felt as Shelly washed off the grime with the piece of strange-smelling soap the woman handed her.

While she tried to shampoo the dirt and vermin from the waves of her long hair, Shelly observed the woman brushing and shaking out Shelly's slacks, sweater and coat.

When she had rinsed her hair as well as possible in the barely lukewarm water, she reached for the threadbare towel folded on a nearby stool.

The woman guard handed her some rough, very plain but clean, underclothes and a pair of socks. Shelly took them gladly.

When she had finished dressing and was pulling her boots on, the woman gave her a short length of red ribbon and a comb, pointing to a cracked mirror on the wall.

As she tried to smooth the tangled curls around her face, she was thankful her hair hadn't been shorn as some of the women's had.

Shelly tied her hair back with the ribbon, gazing startled at her pale reflection, the smudgy shadows beneath her large dark eyes.

The woman ushered her out through the main room of the unit. They followed the now somewhat familiar route through the corridors and upstairs to the dreaded panelled door.

Knocking, the guard opened it and gently pushed her into the room. The door shut softly.

Thankfully, Shelly saw that Victor Varonyuk was not there. Instead, it was Boris Gula who beckoned her from behind the desk to take her seat.

"We are prepared to release you, Prisoner Lee. The car is waiting to take you back to Orensk."

Clutching the arms of the chair, Shelly said nothing, sure her imagination was playing tricks on her.

"Before you leave, there is the matter of your confession. Here; sign."

Wanting with all her heart to take the pen and write her name at the bottom of the page, Shelly hesitated, remembering the retaliations they might take on her relatives and on Demetri.

"Come, come. Time is short. I must insist you sign before you leave."

Very slowly, Shelly shook her head.

Gula's hand clenched; then seeming to recall something himself, he stretched his fingers flat on the desk top as if forcefully holding them there against their wishes.

"You may leave," he said, his strained voice low.

Shelly sat motionless, sure she was hallucinating.

He stood suddenly, shouting an order. The door opened and two young guards entered.

"Now go! You are released! Go!" Gula's voice was harsh. Shelly wondered if he could become violent as Varonyuk had.

She stood up, suddenly feeling almost foolishly brave.

"What are you going to say to the American Embassy when they demand an answer for my illegal imprisonment and treatment?" she asked, facing him across the corner of the desk.

The hardness left his voice. A strange smile slid across his lips, deepening the heavy lines above his jowls.

"Your imprisonment? Were you detained somewhere, young lady? We have no record of you here."

"What?" Shelly gasped. "You know you had me in several cells here. How can you say that?"

"You are mistaken, of course," Gula said. "We know nothing of you. No one here has seen an American girl in our institution. Now go before I change my mind!"

Strong hands of the guards on her arms turned her and guided her out of the room to the carpeted corridor.

Sure it was another of the KGB ploys, Shelly stumbled along, wondering which cell she would get thrown into now.

The heavy door they opened after a short walk led outdoors into a dimly lit courtyard.

The guards escorted her to the backseat of a large black car. One of them got in beside her; the other took the wheel, and soon the dark high walls of the prison were far behind.

The headlights of the big car probed the darkness ahead as they skimmed over the snowy highway.

Still not sure she wasn't dreaming, Shelly relaxed against the seat cushions, her heart breathing a silent prayer, "Thank you, Lord. Thank you, Thank you."

A cluster of lights appeared ahead, and shortly they were on the streets of a small town.

The car pulled to the curb. The guard got out and opened the door, motioning her out. Then the door slammed, the car pulled away.

Looking around the dark street, its only illumination a dim light on the corner and a lighted window nearby, Shelly realized she was standing in front of Pavel's print shop.

Walking to the large front window of the sparsely lighted restaurant, she looked inside but saw no one she knew.

Weak, hungry, and shivering with cold, she was tempted to go inside, but decided against it, feeling suspicious and fearful of everyone.

Knowing the Barinov home was only a few blocks from there, she decided to try to find the way. It was much farther to Aunt Tanya's. Turning, she trudged along the snowy walk, passing darkened stores.

Entering the residential streets, and with the aid of dim moonlight, Shelly soon found the familiar house.

Quickly she climbed the steps of the little house and knocked on the door. In a minute or so, it swung open and tears of relief rushed to her eyes. In the doorway stood Demetri.

His arms reached out, pulling her inside. His tears of joy mingled with hers as he held her close.

"Shelly, Shelly," he murmured. "How did you get here?"

"They brought me to the print shop. I walked from there."

They stood so for a full minute until Galina entered the room to see who had been at the door.

Loving hands removed Shelly's coat and boots, and led her to the warm comfort of the kitchen where supper aromas lingered.

Demetri sat beside her at the table, encircling her with his arm, while Galina hurriedly prepared tea.

Mrs. Barinov, tears glistening on her cheeks, sat across from them slicing bread and cheese and leftover sausage.

They insisted that Shelly not talk until she had eaten.

"You look like a starved little sparrow, Shelly," Galina said, a concerned smile on her face.

Hugging her gently, Demetri whispered close to Shelly's ear, "I was frantic, finding you gone when I returned yesterday."

She told them briefly what had happened to her, omitting the bad parts. Then she rose. "I must get home. Aunt Tanya must be very worried."

"She is," Demetri said. "I intend to take you just as soon as you feel a bit rested. I've been given a car to use for a few days to cover some work in a scattered area. Then I must return to Helsinki for a short time."

"Am I not to see you at all?" Shelly asked, tears filling her eyes.

"Don't worry. We'll arrange some time," Demetri said.

A short while later when Aunt Tanya opened her door, her face shone with rejoicing at seeing Shelly. "Galina phoned to say you had arrived there," she said, her arms around Shelly.

"May I come by early tomorrow morning before I leave for the day?" Demetri asked.

"Have breakfast with us," Aunt Tanya offered.

When he had left, she took an envelope from her pocket, handing it to Shelly.

"A young man brought this to the door this morning. He said his name was Nicoli and rushed away."

The envelope held three small oblongs of paper.

With surprise, Shelly recognized one as the flyleaf of her New Testament with her name written in the corner. The other was the card she'd been using as a bookmark, containing Uncle Vladimer's and Aunt Tanya's names and address.

Shelly slid the third paper from the envelope.

On it was typed a notation:

Kreklon Prison
Comrades Varonyuk and Gula
Punishment cell.

"I told Demetri immediately," Aunt Tanya said. "I was so thankful he had returned home."

With a wondering shake of her head, she added, "I don't know how, but in some way Demetri seems to have arranged your release. When he said he was going to see what he could do, I was afraid they might lock him up, too, for protesting.

"He phoned later to say you were to be released tomorrow morning. What a shock for all of us to see you tonight."

"It was completely unexpected for me, too," Shelly said. She remembered Demetri's connection with the Party and comments he had made to her about illegal black-market activities he knew some officials engaged in. She wondered if it may have been Varonyuk and Gula he knew something about, and had used his knowledge to blackmail them for her freedom.

She went in to hug Aunt Natalia, who, Aunt Tanya said, had been praying almost constantly for Shelly since her disappearance.

Except for a troubling dream, Shelly slept soundly that night for the first time in weeks. She awoke the next morning with thanksgiving to God at finding herself at Aunt Tanya's instead of in a cell.

Demetri arrived carrying a large package of sausages and herring he had purchased while away.

At the breakfast table Shelly asked him, "Why do you have to go to Helsinki when you've just been there?"

"I'm to do a special coverage with a photographer on the pre-wedding days of one of our country's Olympic figure-skating couples. Then we're to cover the wedding in Moscow.

"I was just given the assignment two days ago while doing the story on some amateur competitions of select students from the Leningrad Institute of Physical Culture."

"Will you be taking a train?" Shelly asked.

"I'll drive to Leningrad and take the train from there. Why do you ask?"

"I had a vivid dream last night," Shelly answered. "I realize it was just a dream, but you were on a train that crashed. I was walking in a forest nearby and was trying to hurry through deep snow to help you."

"It *was* just a dream. I'll be fine."

They had a few moments alone at the door as Demetri was leaving. He put his arms around her.

"I was very much tempted to defect from my country several days ago, Shelly. Because of my change in values, I must do that, unless I can figure some way to effectively serve God in the situation I'm presently in.

"I'm sure they will send me away to a labor camp, or worse, when I leave the Party, so my family will be without income anyway until Pavel comes home and can work again.

"I knew I would be with you if I could reach America; also I would have freedom in my writing. But I just couldn't leave my loved ones in trouble."

"I'm glad you feel that way, Demetri. I respect you for it."

"I'll see you tomorrow evening, beloved," Demetri said, kissing her gently and holding her an extra moment.

Shelly spent the intervening daytime hours in the secret room copying with Fyodor and Leonila. Without her Testament, she had to write only a few Scripture verses she had committed to memory, adding a hymn to each page.

During the night, the dream came again: Demetri on a train, the crash, a fire.

As they sat copying the next day, Fyodor shared with her his conviction that he should try to escape to the West with his family, though he had no idea yet as to how to accomplish it.

"As a fugitive in hiding, I'm no good to my congregation anymore," he said.

"And if I'm turned in by someone who may observe me if I start serving as pastor again, my family and many others would certainly be punished.

"As I have prayed, I have felt no leading except that I am to be prepared to leave."

That evening she told Aunt Tanya of Fyodor's concern.

"Yes, we have been praying together about it. I am afraid for them if they leave here. Yet, I know they cannot stay down there forever."

"Fyodor has been a fine, loving pastor, with deep insights into God's Word for one still so young. I am sure the Lord has work for him somewhere.

"I, too, have felt strongly they should try to get away, to another country, perhaps. I'm sure the entire congregation would agree and give them their blessing if they knew."

When Demetri arrived, she told him of these conversations as they strolled along the snowy streets to the little restaurant for dessert together.

"You want to leave, too, Demetri. Is there any possible way

you could go and take them with you?"

"That, Shelly, is just a dream, I'm afraid."

"My dream came again last night," Shelly said. "About you on the train with me walking in a forest along the tracks. The train crashed again, and there was a fire."

"You are probably tense from your time in the prison, Shelly. I'm sure it is no more than that."

But Shelly was beginning to wonder.

When the dream came again that night, her wondering changed to conviction.

"Aunt Tanya," she asked next morning, "do you think God ever tries to tell us something while we're sleeping? As in a dream, maybe?"

"He may. There are such incidents recorded in the Bible, and the Word tells us He is the same, yesterday, today and forever."

"But I've not heard of it happening in recent times, have you?" Shelly persisted.

"I cannot say that for certain, Shelly. There have been times when His voice has spoken definitely to me when I needed guidance. It was not in a dream; but was a silent one inside me, one I knew was His. I'm sure he uses other ways, also."

Shelly awoke in the middle of the night, shaking and perspiring, even in the chilly little bedroom.

It was the dream again, only this time she had recognized the people trudging with her through the forest beside the railroad tracks.

She threw the covers back and went to the window.

Kneeling on the little braided rug, she looked out at a moon that soon would be full again.

"Lord," she prayed softly, "if you are telling me something, give me the dream one more time. And please make a way for me to understand.

"But if I'm just having a recurring nightmare, let me sleep soundly the next few nights. Forgive me if I'm being foolish in asking this."

Shelly knelt there a while longer, calmness stealing over her. Then she slipped back into bed and immediately fell asleep.

The next morning as she was taking breakfast to Fyodor's family, Demetri arrived in a car.

He came down for a brief visit, and Fyodor told him of his strong feeling that he should try to leave the country with his family.

Later, upstairs in the kitchen, Demetri said, "It's a beautiful day, Shelly. The snow is sparkling in the sunshine. Would you enjoy a drive?"

"That sounds like fun. Do you mind, Aunt Tanya?"

"Of course not, dear. Your time here is getting short. Enjoy yourselves together," she said, smiling fondly at them.

"We will stop somewhere for lunch," Demetri said, "and plan to be back midafternoon."

They had barely pulled away from the Rozkalne home when Shelly said, "Demetri, I must talk to you about something."

"Sure," he said, reaching over to grasp her hand, "but why so serious?"

"Because it may be very important. Maybe you can help me figure it out."

Shelly told him briefly of the dream's recurrences and the vividness of the one of the previous night.

"In the dream Fyodor and Leonila were walking with me, and Ivan and little Anna . . . and . . ."

Demetri glanced questioningly at her, "And?"

"Just before the train crashed, I saw it approaching some sort of barricade. There were guards there."

Shelly told him then of waking in terror, and of her request to the Lord.

"And you went back to sleep and slept well, correct?" Demetri asked, smiling gently as he stopped at an intersection leaving Orensk.

"I felt very peaceful," Shelly said, "and went right back to sleep. But the dream started again and I was carrying little Anna through the forest beside the tracks.

"Then the dream changed, and I was looking down on the scene as though it were a game board with a tiny toy train on a maze of tracks.

"At one end was a tiny Russian flag; near the other, a white flag with a horizontal cross in a lovely shade of blue."

"Finland's," Demetri said.

"And at the far end of the game tracks, a tiny replica of America's stars and stripes."

"That's it!" Demetri exclaimed. "But it's too far, too cold."

"What is *it*?" Shelly asked. "And *what's* too far and cold?"

"From the Lord or not, I do not know," Demetri said, "but that may be the way for Fyodor's escape. And ours, too."

Chapter Nineteen

It was late December. As the year neared its end, the country was getting ready for its lavish festivities for the New Year.

Shelly trudged through the snow from the business district, helping Aunt Tanya carry a large fir tree.

As they walked, Shelly expressed surprise that the New Year instead of Christmas is the time of greatest celebration.

"It is because the birth of Christ is ignored by my government," Aunt Tanya said.

"Of course, I didn't think of that."

"In the Soviet calendar, New Year's day is the time set aside to honor the work of the past year, encouraging workers to do even better in the year to come," Aunt Tanya added.

"For many of my people, though, it is also a time of searching for answers to questions in their hearts. They notice that the Christians are joyfully celebrating the birth of Jesus Christ, and they wonder if they are missing a truer meaning for celebration. Often they question us."

"I'm glad you let me pay for the tree, Aunt Tanya. I wanted to get the biggest one possible so we can trim portions off and make a nice little extra tree for Fyodor's family."

"It is a fine idea, Shelly. They will surely appreciate your kind thought and the children will be overjoyed."

"Does the old gentleman, Santa Claus, visit the kids here, or just the Father Frost that Gram told me about?"

Aunt Tanya chuckled. "Here he is Ded Merez, Grandfather Frost, and he comes for the New Year. I have been wondering what I could prepare for Ivan and Anna. I have nothing at all to spend this year."

"I'll help you make some little gifts, Aunt Tanya, and if the stores in Orensk have candy treats, I'll get a few of those."

"Oh, thank you, dear. We are using a lot of your resources, but I accept them in the way I know they are given—in love."

When they reached home they brought the tree into the kitchen. After making sure the doors were locked and securing the shutters on the windows, Shelly went for Fyodor.

Back upstairs, she and Aunt Tanya explained their plans for a December twenty-fifth Christmas. Since Shelly's visa would expire by year's end, they would celebrate on her Christmas.

He entered into their secrets delightedly, anticipating his children's surprise.

While he worked on the tree, Aunt Tanya went for stored decorations.

With borrowed needle and thread and a few malformed branches, Shelly excused herself early that evening and went up to her room.

Laying her wardrobe out on the bed, she checked through it, choosing and discarding.

Around midnight, she smiled with satisfaction at the few items she had completed.

On the chest stood a funny little stuffed-sock horse with stick legs and scarf-fringe mane and tail. On his back sat a twig cowboy wearing an outfit made from denim remnants of Shelly's jeans.

"I'm glad I saved these after I cut book covers from the legs," she mused.

In a quilted-satin bassinette that looked like one of Shelly's slippers minus the heel slept a chubby little nylon doll.

"Never having made one of you before," she said half-aloud, "you turned out surprisingly well, Little One." Rolling a bit of a section of pantyhose, she stuffed a tiny leg.

An hour later she was snipping lace from a slip-hem to attach to a christening-type dress and bonnet she had fashioned from several of Gram's lovely soft old hand-embroidered handkerchiefs.

I brought these to give to great-aunt Natalia, but both she and Gram would agree this is the best use for them under the circumstances, I'm sure.

Before dressing the cunning little baby, Shelly cut off a length of her own curly brown hair and stitched it to the tiny head.

When the little one was in dress and bonnet, the idea came.

Snapping a couple of branches into various lengths, she laid them aside ready for the next morning, Christmas Eve Day.

After their breakfast, Aunt Tanya searched out some pieces of discarded dresses from her remnant bag, and by afternoon Shelly had assisted Ivan and Anna in making a group of crude but colorfully dressed stick-figure wisemen and shepherds who stood around the nylon baby in its slipper bed.

"They are the nicest, most lovingly made ones I've ever seen," she said as the youngsters placed them under the decorated tree in the secret room.

Leonila smiled. "I told them this is your Christmas Eve, and they have been pestering to go upstairs this evening to look out a window and watch for the first evening star. It is one of our traditions here on Christmas Eve."

Demetri arrived, two days ahead of schedule, loaded down with bags containing herring and cheeses, breads, candy and wrapped gifts.

"Shelly had said she wished she could have a Christmas observance on the twenty-fifth, so I decided to get back by then if at all possible," he said, grinning at Aunt Tanya as she let him in the door.

Shelly ran from the kitchen and hugged him, packages and all.

"I'm so glad you're here! I didn't expect you."

"Me too," he said. "It's so good to see you.

"I wrote up the pre-wedding weekend and then got all the information I needed from the wedding party the day before the marriage. I didn't want to be away that extra day or so. My heart was here. I wanted to be here with you."

He put the food bags down on the table and headed back into the parlor with the one full of brightly wrapped packages.

"We're having the celebration down with Fyodor's family. But Aunt Tanya felt we should put a tree here, too, as usual, so it would appear that everything was going on normally."

"Yes," Aunt Tanya said, "we will try to keep up appearances even with Vladimer and Valentina away, so as to not draw attention to our home."

"I think that is best," Demetri said.

"I brought things to make borcht, macka, veranyahet, cucha and kimfut, too, if you have time to prepare them, Tanya," Demetri said. "I'll make time," she answered smiling. "Then Shelly can taste some of our traditional holiday dishes."

"And I brought kolach," he said, pulling a large loaf of bread from its wrapping. A piece of golden wheat was affixed to its top, centered with a chunky red candle.

"The candle reminds me of Christmas Eve candlelight Communion services on Christmas Eve at home," Shelly said.

"So also do we," Aunt Tanya said, "but this year without my Valentina and Vladimer, and our pastor not able to lead us, how different it will be."

"But," Demetri said, "since it is the date of Shelly's Christmas, and the pastor is in your cellar, we could have a special service tonight, even though we would only be part of the local congregation."

Aunt Tanya smiled through her tears. "A fine thought, Demetri. Vladimer has always been responsible for the church's Communion wine. It is stored down there in a special crate. I will make the bread immediately."

Her spirits seemed to perk up, and she said, "Shelly, in the top shelf of the little parlor cabinet are some tiny crystal goblets given to me years ago by a wealthy lady for whom I worked. You get them, please, and the silver platter wrapped in flannel next to them."

The secret room was as reverent as a cathedral to the small group gathered together that evening.

Candles set in the niches in the wall, flanking the Communion articles on the rough table, cast soft flickering shadows over the faces of the people seated on the cots.

Ivan and Anna tried to sit quietly, their mother's stern shake of the head keeping their exuberance in check.

And as they were eating, Jesus took bread, and blessed it, and broke it, and gave it to the disciples, and said, Take, eat; this is my body. And he took the cup, and gave thanks, and gave it to them, saying, Drink ye all of it; For this is my blood . . . which is shed for many. . . .

"For those in prison today for their love of Thee, our God," Fyodor prayed, "we ask for them strength and courage to share their faith. They had counted the cost of serving you, Lord Jesus, and decided it was worth the suffering.

"May we here be as strong. Show us what to do that we may not fail you in your plans for us."

To his tiny congregation, Fyodor said, "Answers to our prayers often come more speedily than we dare to expect. Believe in our God. Be prepared for His answers."

As Shelly was climbing the narrow stairs to the kitchen behind Aunt Tanya, she heard Demetri say, "Keep up the training you said you have been doing to build up your endurance, Fyodor. Involve Leonila and the children if you have not already. You will need all the stamina you can muster. God willing, your escape to freedom is near."

Aunt Tanya went into her mother's room to tend to her needs before she went to her own bed, while Demetri closed the trapdoor and replaced the rug and table.

Shelly said, "I'm glad Fyodor came up for a Communion service with Aunt Natalia before we had ours.

"She must have noticed my concern for her frailness because afterward she said to me through Aunt Tanya that 'death does not seem dark and frightening to me, because it is my gateway to heaven.' "

Demetri nodded. "I think about that reason in regard to our Christian relatives and friends in prison. Your Uncle Vladimer said that the persecution is purifying the Church and burning away the chaff. The persecutors don't realize that they are making us stronger and more determined, and that killing us will only release us to a better life."

"I've learned," Shelly said, "in the weeks here what it can mean to really love the Lord. I hope I never let the complexities of daily life diminish this realization."

"I'm sure you won't, Shelly," he said, hugging her.

Taking a small velvet box from his pocket, he pressed it into her hand. "I will go now. I know you and your aunt will be very busy preparing for your Christmas dinner, and I've not been home yet to see what Galina and Mother may need."

As he went out the door, he added, "Open it in the morning. I'll see you around noon."

Shelly put the little box under her pillow that night, tempted to pull off the curled white ribbon and peek inside the lid, but she waited with anticipation until the morning.

Excitement kept waking her, so at 4 a.m., snapping on the light, she said to herself, "Well, it *is* morning."

Slipping the ribbon off the soft velvet of the box, she found inside the lid a folded piece of paper. "My heart desired to give you a ring as a pledge of my wish to marry you. Because of uncertainties facing us, I present this for now—a token of my love, which is yours, as long as we both shall live. . . . Demetri."

Tears overflowing her eyes, love for Demetri filling her heart, Shelly held in her palm a tiny silver heart on a thin silver chain.

Centered on the heart sparkled a diamond shaped like a minute teardrop.

Slipping the chain over her head, concealing the heart inside the neckline of her gown, she whispered, "Forever, Demetri; as long as we both shall live."

Chapter Twenty

Aunt Natalia was sound asleep when Shelly went in to dress her in a pretty shawl and gown in preparation for Demetri's carrying her down the cellar stairs for the Christmas dinner.

So, instead, they carried down the remaining dishes that were wafting delicious aromas throughout the house.

The secret room was festive, filled with the children's delighted laughter and chatter.

When plates were filled, Fyodor stood to ask God's blessing on the meal.

"Our Heavenly Father, we—"

Bang! Thud! They heard pounding on the front door and loud voices uttering commands.

"Take your plates! Quickly! Upstairs!" Demetri whispered sharply to Shelly and Aunt Tanya. "And a cheese and a loaf of bread!"

Ivan and Anna stared with tears filling their eyes as the two women disappeared from the room.

Demetri grabbed his plate and using his free hand, positioned the bedspring over the opening, throwing and kicking straw against it.

The trapdoor was closed, and the rug replaced, and the table positioned with their filled plates on it.

As Demetri and Shelly slid into chairs, Aunt Tanya ran to open the door.

Feigning ignorance of their presence, Tanya looked past the two uniformed men on the porch to her neighbor standing on the sidewalk.

"Why, Sergie Sokolov," she said loudly in English, "do come in. We are celebrating her Christmas with my American niece who is visiting."

Then, as though just noticing them, she looked questioningly at the other two men on the porch.

Taken aback during the moments she had spoken to Sokolov, they now pushed past her into the parlor.

Glancing briefly at the tree and gifts, they went into the kitchen. Shelly and Demetri looked up from their plates, and Shelly stood, smiling in greeting, motioning them to sit at the table.

Seemingly nonplused for a few moments, they stared strangely at Demetri.

Then, evidently letting the aromas and laden plates sway their decision, the young men accepted the offered chairs. Removing their coats, hats and gloves, they sat down, grinning in appreciation.

Grateful that there was still ample food remaining in the cooking pots, Shelly got up to prepare plates for them, and Aunt Tanya bustled about preparing tea.

Practicing their English in conversation with Shelly, the two men became jovial, eating their unexpected feast with relish. Sokolov, looking scared at this turn of events, hurried away.

Following third cups of tea after their meal was finished, the men left, apologizing profusely to Shelly for interrupting her festivities and thanking her for inviting them.

The smile abruptly left Demetri's face when the door had shut after them. "We must not delay in getting Fyodor out of here. People are getting too suspicious."

Aunt Tanya returned from locking the front door, "Since Sokolov, my next-door neighbor, is evidently the informer, we have no way of knowing what he may have observed."

"I made plans while in Helsinki," Demetri said very quietly. "You remember, Shelly, I spoke of the married couple who led me to the knowledge of the Lord?"

Shelly nodded.

"They will be the connection," Demetri said. "If we can get Fyodor's family that far, they will get him to safety."

"But how will we do that?" Shelly asked.

"You gave me the idea, or your dream did. Let's go downstairs, and I'll lay it out before Fyodor and Leonila."

To keep them occupied, Ivan and Anna were allowed to open their gifts.

An hour later the decision had been made to leave in four days. There was much to be done in the meantime.

When Aunt Tanya, Demetri and Shelly left for his home late in the afternoon, they gave the appearance of going to a party. All three carried to the car bags filled with some of the Tens family's clothing, wrapped at the bag tops in the discarded gift wrappings and ribbons.

That night was cloudy and moonless. Shelly and Demetri took a chance and carried Ivan and Anna to the car, thence to the Barinov home.

Very early in the morning, on December twenty-eighth, Fyodor, disguised in a woman's clothes and shawl, carrying a net bag as though going shopping, walked the snowy blocks to the deserted park where Demetri picked him up in the car.

Late in the afternoon, Leonila, dressed in Aunt Tanya's old coat and shawl, which were familiar in the immediate neighborhood, walked the same route with Shelly to Demetri's cruising car. His home became their temporary sanctuary.

Well after dark on the twenty-ninth with supplies in the trunk and Fyodor's family hidden under a blanket in the back of the car, Demetri and Shelly began the long drive to Karonlac, a town about twenty miles from the border.

"There's no way to get you closer without passes for everyone, which of course is impossible," Demetri said.

"Are you sure, Shelly, that you wouldn't rather take the train?"

"I've thought about it a lot," she answered. "I know the long walk won't be easy in the deep snow and cold. But I can be a help to Leonila and Fyodor. Anna and Ivan will probably have to be carried much of the way, and Fyodor may still be weak."

"I suppose you're right. But I feel guilty, planning to take the train when the rest of you will be walking."

"But you have to get there ahead of time on the train in order to help us if we make it across the border," Shelly said.

"Yes, I know. We won't be expected this soon. I had made tentative plans with my friends for a month from now, and I've not been able to contact them to change the date."

"Well, I'm thankful you were able to get permission to leave the country again so soon," she said.

Demetri chuckled, "If the head of the Writers Union Exit Commission hadn't wanted some items brought in for him, I probably wouldn't have. I'm not sure how I'll fit them all in my suitcase. And if he doesn't meet me at customs to clear my way in, I'll have a big problem."

"Then you've definitely decided to not go the rest of the way with us?" she asked, deep disappointment in her voice.

"I've made preparation so I may, if I decide it seems the right time. Except for some funds I have with me for the trip, I've opened an account for Galina and Mother with all my savings, so I could leave knowing they would have food and other necessities."

"I'm glad you did that, Demetri. If you get into America, I'm sure you'd find a good position with your writing experience."

"Yes, I feel confident about that. It's leaving my country and my family that would be difficult. But knowing they are all right financially for a short while will lessen the burden. I had not thought earlier about shifting my savings, and had only considered their need for regular income if I were to leave or were imprisoned and were not working here."

"And there seems nothing anyone can do to lessen the persecution, Demetri," Shelly said, hope beginning to rise in her heart. "You need to get away, too. You said you'll probably face prison when you renounce the Party."

Demetri's hand left the wheel and held hers tightly for a moment, "And you would be my family in America. Is that not right?"

"Yes, Demetri," Shelly leaned across the bundle on the seat between them and stroked his cheek.

An hour later, they stopped in a secluded area near a clump of trees to let Fyodor's family have a short reprieve from their cramped positions.

When they continued on, Ivan and Anna sat in front between Demetri and Shelly.

Before midnight they had swung onto a secondary road around the outskirts of Leningrad, and had been stopped only once for the checking of Internal Passes. Satisfied with Demetri's pass, the policeman didn't bother asking about Shelly's, evidently assuming they were a young family.

At dawn they were eating a meal of bread and cheese, parked along a wayside road at the edge of a forest.

"The important thing to remember," Demetri said, "is to keep the railroad tracks in sight, so you don't get lost. You should reach them by daylight. And during the day, travel inside the forest, just far enough so you won't be seen. There are enough evergreen trees to enable you to move unobserved if you are very watchful."

After checking the small backpacks the three adults were wearing, and shaking Fyodor's and Leonila's hands, he put his arms around Shelly.

"You may be risking your life, beloved. I am proud of you. I would not let you do it if we did not feel so strongly our God's leading."

Then, holding her face between his hands, he kissed her.

"I have no idea how you can possibly get across the border, except that it will then be New Year's Eve, and quite probably the guards will have been drinking and not expecting problems.

"Remember, there is no shame in turning back if you must.

"I will be in the last car of the train to Helsinki that should cross the border around midnight. My friends and I will backtrack and wait for you just beyond the border, northwest of the last patrol tower. There is a small road running near the edge of the cleared area."

"Demetri," Shelly said softly, "if I do not see you again, if you do not get to America, or in case I do not make it—"

Shelly paused, choking back a sob, "Know that I love you."

He held her close a few moments, then stood watching as they left the road and entered the edge of the forest.

Holding Anna's hand, Shelly turned as she heard the car door slam. She watched the taillights disappear, and felt as though her heart were breaking.

They walked until dusk when, after sighting the tracks, they wrapped in blankets and huddled together in a small snow-cleared area under the low branches of a large fir tree, sleeping that night before continuing on.

All the next day they trudged through the snow, stopping only for short rest periods, eating bread and cheese around noon.

By early nightfall they were exhausted. A sign along a little-used road showed them it was still five miles to the border.

An abandoned shed offered shelter. "We will sleep a few hours," Fyodor said, putting Anna down on a tree stump and trying the shed door.

"There will be little moonlight again tonight. Still we can make our way, and we need not be so fearful when we enter the forbidden zone of being observed."

Leonila sat down beside Anna. "The few people who live in the zone, acting as guards, will probably all be celebrating tonight anyway, and will not be as watchful."

"We will hope so," Fyodor said. "But our God has brought

us this far. We will each continue praying each step of the way and trust Him."

When they awoke, snow was swirling gently down. They resumed their trek, seeing pinpoints of light far in the distance.

"Evidently the border station for the train," Fyodor explained. "We will head in that general direction."

"It is so dark, no one can see us," Leonila said. "Can we not walk along this little road adjacent to the tracks? It would be so much easier, Fyodor, than struggling through the drifts of snow."

As they hiked along quickly through the darkness, the points of light slowly increased in size, reminding them that just before them was safety or defeat.

Later, when Shelly shined her tiny flashlight momentarily on her watch, she saw it was almost eleven o'clock.

They trudged along, and after a while, anticipation rising in her as she knew it must be in Leonila and Fyodor, Shelly checked her watch again. It was eleven fifty-five.

The lights were close now, perhaps just a mile away.

Then in the distance, Shelly heard the approaching train. She wished she could know if Demetri was really on it. She wanted to be assured of his nearness, that his plans for all of them were so far working well.

The roaring, pulsating sound of the train was close now.

"Quickly, behind those trees over there," Fyodor whispered loudly.

But Shelly ducked down behind a pile of logs scattered along the track.

The train rocketed by, an engine and three cars. She had a fleeting glimpse of Demetri in the last car staring out into the darkness, probably wondering where they were.

With a shock, Shelly realized the train wasn't slowing for the stop ahead. Surely it would have to stop for the bordercheck, even on New Year's Eve.

Sudden fear gripped her as she remembered the sharp jog of the tracks she had asked Demetri about on the trip to Leningrad the day she had arrived from America.

It was the jog where Demetri had said, "The engineer knows that if he doesn't slow to a crawl, they'll never make it."

Shelly knew in that split second that for the rest of her life she would remember that scream of metal on metal.

Horrible sounds of a thunderous crashing beat against her ears.

Then silence. Utter silence.

Shelly saw that the tracks were as clear as if a train had never been there moments before.

But alongside the tracks lay a mass of twisted, steaming metal.

From somewhere in the depths of the wreckage a flame licked forth, hesitated, licked again, and began quickly moving along from the engine to the cars.

In horror, Shelly slipped the straps of the backpack from her shoulders and started to run. Her legs moved, her arms pumped, as in a slow-motion dream.

Her breath tore at her aching throat as she ran praying from her heart, "Please, God. Demetri."

Shelly was unaware of Fyodor panting along behind her, or of Leonila following, dragging Ivan and Anna along the snowy road.

In those moments, their own safety had been somehow forgotten.

Their whole beings were projected forward to the tragedy ahead.

In the swirling snow, the scene to Shelly seemed like a dream. Surely it couldn't be reality—running, running, running, terror pulling at her.

Then she was there.

She clambered across the tracks and down the embankment.

Moans and screams, and cries for help propelled her onward. She must find Demetri!

She saw men running up the track from the guardhouse. When they reached the cars, Shelly saw that they were unsteady and disoriented.

Drunk, probably, she thought, disgust shoving aside part of her fear for a moment. *Lot of help they'll be.*

She squirmed her way through a collapsed narrow door into the last car.

Demetri, groggy but unhurt except for a gash on his cheek was crawling along the slanting floor trying to help the seriously injured.

Shelly saw many were dead or unconscious. She helped Demetri out of the car, then went back to assist several others who could walk or crawl.

She saw Fyodor coming from the next car, pulling out an injured man.

The border guards seemed now to have been shocked into complete awareness. They, too, were working frantically to remove the rest of the passengers before the approaching flames reached them.

A large number of passengers from the other cars were miraculously uninjured, but seemed in a daze, milling about where Leonila stood with Ivan and Anna. Both youngsters were crying in fear at the spectacle.

Seeing Shelly, Leonila came to where she was just as a guard strode up, saying something to Shelly.

Leonila whispered quickly, "He's commending you for not panicking after the crash, and for helping your fellow passengers."

Shelly smiled and nodded at him as he moved on to where Fyodor and another guard were helping the last persons from the twisted middle car.

"Your clothes are covered with blood and dirt," Leonila said as they stood in the cold with the passengers, watching the flames completely enveloping the train.

Shelly smiled. "I'm so glad we got here in time to help. For all your husband's been through, he's shown unexpected strength."

"Surely, God was with us," Leonila said, as Fyodor joined them. He sat down on the snowy embankment, too weary to stand.

"The guard who was helping me with those last two people said he phoned for ambulances before running over here. They think the engineer was drunk, and that's why he didn't slow for the curve. The guard is going back now to order an extra train to take us all on to Helsinki.

"He said two guards will accompany us to explain the lack of papers for most of us due to the fire."

The four of them, Shelly and Demetri, Fyodor and Leonila, looked at each other, tears coursing down their cheeks amid the dirt and snowflakes, the comprehension of what God had accomplished for their escape filling their hearts with awe.

Joining hands in a circle around Ivan and Anna, they bowed their heads. Standing in the freezing cold amid the crowd of people, the little group silently gave thanks to God.

Far in the distance they heard church bells still ringing in the new year.

"Shelly," Fyodor said gravely, "when you are home in America, remember that the persecutions of the Christians here are not only from a political force.

"They stem from something more serious, the spiritual illness, the darkness, of those denying God. They have eyes that do not see, ears that do not hear.

"Each time you read your Bible, may your heart weep for those here who do not have one.

"Please, do not forget us.

"Pray for us."

Chapter Twenty-One

Hours later, in Finland, Demetri phoned his friend. Then after a brief visit to the American Embassy, Shelly was with him in the Marlison's comfortable apartment.

Following baths and naps, they sat refreshed at the table that evening enjoying a leisurely dinner and pleasant fellowship.

"I know most people won't believe us when we tell them how we happened to get here," Shelly commented.

"Why is it, I wonder," Greta said, "that we find it difficult to believe God sometimes works things out as He did in the Bible accounts? How shallow our faith must seem to Him."

"But we know it's true," Demetri said. "And Fyodor's family is safe. How glad I am that your embassy has given them temporary asylum and will consider his case."

"I am glad, too, that the embassy agreed to let you stay with us an extra day, Shelly," Greta said, smiling at her.

"Well, they understood about the train crash," Shelly said. "And my visa was good through today anyway.

"I decided to not mention my imprisonment just yet. I know it might put pressure on the Soviet government to let up on the Christians. But I'm afraid they'd only make a pretense of doing so, and instead there would be reprisals, especially for those who knew me there."

"And you, Demetri," Olaf said, slapping him fondly on the shoulder. "You have decided to apply for asylum at the American Embassy, yes?"

Demetri said nothing, looking pensively at Shelly.

"Tell him, yes, Demetri," Shelly said happily. "Tell him."

Slowly Demetri shook his head.

"No, Shelly. I have decided I must go back for a while and make sure there's nothing more for me to do in my country."

"But the Lord gave you a logical way of leaving when He prepared for the Tens' escape."

Shelly felt panic mounting. "Please, Demetri. If you return now you may never have another chance!"

"I'll try for a visa through the Writers' Union as I did this time, or I'll wait until I have another assignment here."

"But if they discover you had part in Fyodor's escape, you won't stand a chance of staying out of prison, will you?"

"There is no reason for them to suspect me, Shelly."

Demetri put his arm around her as she started to say something further.

"No, Shelly. I feel this is something I must do."

"But our place is together. Please, Demetri." Shelly's voice was choked with tears.

In answer, he leaned over and stopped her words with a gentle kiss.

Two days later, before their final goodbye near the American Airlines departing gate at Helsinki's airport, he said, "I will come as soon as I feel the time is right for me.

"When you receive a message saying, 'There is a song, Your People Shall Be My People,' know that I am preparing to make the break. If my attempt is successful, I'll contact you a week or so later, and we will be together."

"Yes, Demetri," Shelly said, holding him tightly, "together, as long as we both shall live."

Epilogue

It was a cold, windy, mid-February afternoon in Chicago.

Shelly's heart was heavy as she walked down Michigan Avenue after work, glancing in the windows decorated with red hearts and lavish, sentimental cards.

She had heard nothing from Demetri and worried that he may have been arrested.

A letter, minus any censoring, had recently reached her from Aunt Tanya. It reminded Shelly that life was going on there, too. Day by day visitors to Russia were seeing "business as usual" in the cities and villages on their tour itineraries, churches open in the Intourist-guided routes, people obviously free to do as they wished. But underneath the pretentions, the Party reigned.

Dear Shelly,

Mother died shortly after your departure. Her funeral was opportunity for a fine, extended church service. A church building was loaned to us; many sermons were preached.

My little Valentina is home, thin and ill, but we are grateful to be together.

My dear Vladimer is being sent into exile in a remote region for five years. Sometimes the family is allowed to accompany the exiled one; we have petitioned to go with him, so our family may be united.

Thank you for your loving visit here.

We here are as in 2 Cor. 4:9 —persecuted, but not forsaken; cast down, but not destroyed.

Aunt Tanya

By early summer the air already felt oppressive, with heat waves rising from Chicago's pavements.

Entering the vestibule of her apartment house, Shelly removed a sheaf of mail from her box.

"So much junk mail all the time," she muttered.

Unlocking her door, she sank wearily on the couch, dropping her purse and mail beside her.

She missed Demetri so much, and her aching heart was beginning to believe she would never see him again.

Listlessly leafing through the pile of circulars, she jerked upright as a postcard with a foreign postmark fell from a magazine.

Eagerly, she picked it up, her heart fluttering with anticipation.

I was in Moscow in early June when the lilacs were blooming.
Their sweetness reminded me of you.
All is well.
Have you heard . . . there is a song,
Your People Shall Be My People?